About the author

Ajay K Pandey is currently working with Cognizant, Pune. Although he grew up with a dream of becoming a teacher, destiny landed him in the IT field. Travelling, trekking and reading novels are his hobbies. Travelling to different places has taught him about different cultures and people, and makes him wonder how despite all the differences, there is a bond that unites them. Trekking always inspires him to deal with challenges like a sport.

Reading is perhaps what makes him feel alive. Apart from writing, he wants to follow his role model Mother Teresa and make some contribution to the society.

His debut novel *You are the Best Wife* was based on his life events and went on to become a bestseller soon after its release. It charmed many hearts and inspired several others to live every moment with love, peace and happiness.

You can know more about him and his books on:

f /AuthorAjayPandey

🐦 @AjayPandey_08

or write to him at ajaypandey0807@gmail.com.

000000128292

Her Last Wish

Ajay K Pandey

Srishti
PUBLISHERS & DISTRIBUTORS

SRISHTI PUBLISHERS & DISTRIBUTORS
Registered Office: N-16, C.R. Park
New Delhi – 110 019
Corporate Office: 212A, Peacock Lane
Shahpur Jat, New Delhi – 110 049
editorial@srishtipublishers.com

First published by
Srishti Publishers & Distributors in 2017

Printed and bound in India

Dedicated to my HIV friend.
I wish I could mention your name.

"Always try to represent yourself as 'happy',
because, initially it becomes your 'look',
gradually it becomes your 'habit',
and one day, it becomes your 'personality'."
— *Astha Sharma*

A note from the author

When I started writing my first book *You are the Best Wife*, I never had, even in my wildest dreams, imagined that it will win so many hearts. I just did a little research on my own to find out what works in the market, read a few dozen books and realized that readers are unpredictable, that there are no flat rules. So I made a rule for myself – I will write like a husband, not a writer. This could have been my first and last book, but whenever I decided to quit, I got a review which said, 'you have come so far… you did it in the past, and you can do it again'. I try to reply to every single message and comment that I get. Believe it or not, it is you who has made me what I am today. I would take this opportunity to thank all the wonderful hearts who stood in my support in their own individualistic way. Your reviews and feedback are the silent way to promote an author, especially one who have limited resources to promote a book. I would like to thank the following readers who have now become a part of my life, my extended family – Sheetal Poojari, Anandhini Iyappan, Lalita Sharma, Rajesh D. Hajare, Ranjithakrishna Mudradi, VP Dharshini Vellingiri, Huma Naaz, VishakhaTiwari, Anupama Sudhir Singh, Riya Ranjan, Nivetha Muralidharan, Shweta Desai, Sunaina Kapoor, Satish P Babu, Monika Pandya, Nidha Mohan, Madhu Shunmuganathan, Pallav Goswami, Tania Chatterjee, Guru Priya, Merlin Felisha, Arpita Saxena, and ChocoHolic Angellina.

Special thanks to Subhajit Das who has read *You are the Best Wife* almost two hundred times. (Unbelievable!)

Thank you Jayantakumar Bose and Arup Bose for standing up for me when everyone else denied.

Thanks to my editor friend Stuti Sharma for getting rid of the unwanted words and making the book a beautiful read.

Special thanks to Kanishka Gupta from Writer's Side for guiding me through the publishing process. And, most importantly, Vishal Anand, a dear friend, who tells me what works and what doesn't since the pre-order of my debut book. I owe it to you, man!

Thanks to Madhuri Varma, Ankit Bhan and Ravi Kant Gautam for their contribution in the book.

So, here is my second book! No matter how many books I write, *You are the Best Wife* would always be close to my heart.

What I am today is because of a beautiful soul who made me a better person. Now onwards, a portion of my royalty will always go for donation. I refrain to mention any fixed percentage as readers will make their own opinion about me and I don't want to use this as an appeal to sell my books.

Thank you for making me an author, though I would politely say – I am not an author, nor a celebrity; I am just a husband, who wrote something from his heart.

Never Surrender!

Ajay

1

There are three kinds of teachers in this world – those who teach what they feel like teaching; those who teach what students want them to teach; and those who intend to teach, but never really do. I happen to fall in the third category.

My salary slip stated my designation as assistant professor, but throughout the year, I was busy invigilating exams, assisting in placements, cultural and technical festivals, counselling students, addressing RTI notices, writing false stories to be published in the college's yearly magazine and making arrangements for a professional tour for students. If I had some time left, I would teach.

I am, in fact, an ad hoc faculty; I am only required to fill in for faculties on leave. Most of my students love me, perhaps because I am a jack of all trades, but essentially, master of none.

Tuesday, June 2010

I disembarked the Goa express at Hazrat Nizamuddin railway station in Delhi after a long journey of thirty-two hours, though I didn't look even half as tired. Delhi was boiling at this time of the year, as if the sun was taking revenge from the Delhiites. Clouds were giving a false ray of hope for rain, by making the air humid. The roads were jam packed with commuters. I managed to hire an auto for Malviya Nagar and after another thirty minutes, just when I was about to press the doorbell of flat no. 65 of block L, the most amazing lady of my life opened the door.

"Good morni..." Even before I could finish, she jumped forward and kissed me. I wasn't surprised because I know she can even climb up the Qutub Minar to exhibit her emotions. I couldn't reciprocate, more concerned about a free show for the oldies doing yoga in the society garden. So I barged inside the house, holding her, and needless to mention, we kissed. This time I reciprocated deeply and passionately. I had explored that a long time gap in two kisses increases its importance manifold.

"I missed you darling!" she whispered in a nasal tone, perhaps because of her cold. I smiled at her and after a few minutes of silent hugging and kissing, murmured slowly, 'Missed you too.' She was elated, because I am not very verbal with my feelings otherwise.

We cuddled in silence for a while. Sometimes, silence speaks a lot and that was the best language known to me. I had been away from home for more than twenty days for the first time after marriage.

"How was the trip?" she asked, caressing my face.

"I was on duty."

"Okay! I know what that means. It was a trip for the students and not for me." She always understood what I meant, and had the audacity to speak for me. I smiled but chose not to speak.

She rose to her feet and said, "Listen, there is poha in the sauce pan and juice in the fridge. Please have your breakfast."

"Where are you going?" I asked instinctively.

"Just in case you have forgotten, I work with Axis bank."

"Why not take the day off, sweetheart? You still have a bad cold," I finally managed to speak my heart. The truth behind me asking her to stay back was that I had missed her badly in the past twenty days. Too add to that the fact that she had the same symptoms when I had left Delhi and she wasn't okay as yet. But Astha rejected my request.

"No," she replied as she brushed her hair. "My probation is due next week and I don't want to give the manager a chance to pull me down. Don't worry, it's just a common cold."

Astha was a career oriented woman, and wanted to make it big in her job. She had a terrible boss, but our financial condition made her stick to the job. I am just an adhoc faculty at Sri Ram College of Art, Science and Commerce.

I walked her to the parking lot and helped her get the Activa out. She was about to drive off when I said, "Do call me before leaving office. I may go to see Papa."

"You usually meet Papa on Saturdays…it is just Tuesday."

"I was away for almost a month."

"I know, I know. You are a son too," she taunted and I smiled.

●

I was exhilarated to be home. It hardly matters whether we stay in a five star hotel or are on a leisure tour, nothing can be compared to the comfort of one's home. I finished my morning chores and was planning to take a short nap, unaware that the very next moment would change the course of my life. It was the moment of truth for me. I wish I could go back in time and never receive that call. It was an unknown landline number.

"Hello," I said.

"Hello, we are calling from Rotary Club blood bank. May I speak with Mrs Astha please?"

"Astha is at work. I am her husband. You may leave your message with me."

"May I know your name, sir?" the lady on the other side sounded serious.

"Vijay Sharma. What is the matter? Is everything okay?"

An awkward silence followed. The lady on the call sighed, giving me an intuition of some bad news. "Mr Vijay," she finally said, "since you are her husband and our records confirm your name as her family member, please understand that it is not our duty to inform you and that we may be incorrect in our understanding." A long pause followed.

"What is the matter? Please come to the point." I was getting restless.

"Your wife had donated blood during a blood donation camp at her office and as per our standard procedure, we conducted some basic tests such as HIV, p24 antigen and rapid tests. I am extremely sorry to inform you that Mrs Astha Sharma's blood has been diagnosed positive for HIV."

Did she actually say HIV?

It took me a while to register what I had heard. I gathered my wits and said, "If this is some kind of prank call, end it right away!"

I was about to disconnect the call when she said, "This is not a prank call, Mr Vijay. Sir, we are not a hundred percent sure about our diagnosis and would suggest that your wife get the Western Blot test done."

I went numb and lost my voice. Soon I realized that this was happening for real. The word HIV heavily echoed in my head.

"Mr Vijay, are you there?" she prodded as I was lost in my agony and hadn't spoken a single word.

I managed to utter, "HIV... meaning AIDS?"

2

I had heard the unexpected. It was something that I had heard of only on Doordarshan advertisements. Was it the news that could change my fate? Well, that was not the only struggle I had been through.

I had been a loser all my life. People usually say that change is the only constant. But not for me. The only consistent thing in my life was losing.

My grades in school were consistent between forty and fifty percent. Somehow my life had never crossed the threshold of fifty percent. I had prepared for five years for IAS/PCS. I surprised myself for having spent five years for these exams. My father was always hopeful that his son will be an IAS officer someday. It was his craziness to expect something of that kind from me. I am the only child of my parents and considered it to be my moral duty to fulfil my parents' dreams.

After graduating in English from Allahabad University, I had applied for my Master's. During those days, I was also preparing for the IAS exam. I am unsure whether it could be called preparation, but I was sure then and I am sure now that the IAS is beyond my capacity. However, it took five attempts for my father to realize the same thing. I don't blame him for that either, because it was by mistake and I still wonder how I cleared the prelims and main examination of PCS once, which had added two extra years of hope for my father.

I had applied for many government jobs and successfully managed to clear a few written exams as well. The most horrifying part of my life was facing an interview – when five pairs of eyes stare at a person as if they are about to post-mortem him, it becomes difficult for the person to even open his mouth.

At the age of thirty, I realized that I wouldn't be eligible for any government job anymore. I never had a dream of my own to chase, but for my father, his dream of seeing me as a government officer finally died.

I had no courage in me to appear for a recruitment process. How could a mother not sense her child's feelings! She acted as my saviour, declaring that her son wouldn't prepare for any of those stupid exams. A mother's heart always beats for her son, no matter how useless that son is!

My journalist mother helped me to get the job of an Asst. Professor in Sriram College of Arts, Science and Commerce. It was really embarrassing for me that even at the age of thirty, I had to use my mom's reference, and that too for an ad-hoc job. But I had no other choice.

Generally, parents are at peace once their kid settles down in his professional life. But my parents were more worried after my appointment, for the next question was – who would marry such a loser?

I vividly remember the day when Papa had asked me about the kind of girl I was looking for. That was indeed a difficult question. I applied my mind and in the end asked him to decide for me. How could I have made the most important decision of my life when all the other decisions had been made by them? I wonder why he had even asked me. I soon got the answer when my mother asked me whether I had a girlfriend.

I rarely laugh and that was one of those rare moments. My mother too joined me in the laughter, although our reasons were quite different. She was laughing at herself for having asked that question. Who would want to be in love with a person like me, I thought. I am good looking, but again, that was according to my mom. The truth is that I am a boring person. Sometimes some people use good words to say it and cover up by calling me shy instead.

My parents always drifted in opposite directions for everything, but were always united in their views for two reasons: One, they both love me, and two, they both wanted me to settle down and get married to a good girl. I don't blame them for their expectations; after all, every parent has the right to dream of a beautiful daughter-in-law.

An extraordinary profile with fancy details was created on online matchmaking forums. Brahmin boy of height five feet eight inches, fair complexion, smart, age twenty-nine, full-time professor at Sriram College, father works in the police department, mother is a senior editor of a famous newspaper, own house, et al. I hated most of the above mentioned details as I knew the truth of it all, but liked the last line which was in bold – **No Dowry**.

After reading this advertisement on Shaadi.com, I confronted my mother, "Mom, this ad is full of lies."

"What lies?" she asked.

"Everything. My height is five feet seven inches. My age is thirty. I am just an assistant professor and whose house are you referring to as 'own house'?"

"Vijay, isn't this your house too?"

"It suggests as if I am the owner of a separate house."

"You don't worry about all these things. Leave it to me." This is how my parents behaved. Whenever things go complex, they declare that I should leave it to them.

"You mentioned that my complexion is fair. My photo will prove otherwise."

"That is not a lie!" she protested in a serious tone. Her raised voice silenced me.

A year passed by, but my age in the matrimony site remained twenty-nine. As if my mother had taken an oath to promote my age to thirty only once I got married. I met almost a dozen girls; a few showed a little interest in me, but later denied the proposal. Some would ask me to meet them at a nearby mall, few would talk to me over the phone, and we even went to the homes of a few. But each one of them declined eventually.

Whomsoever I met personally, I would tell them that I was not a rich guy and that I was just an ad hoc assistant professor. That would help them in making their decision, but it wasn't helping my family. Every girl had her own reservations – some didn't want to live with my parents while some were looking for a government officer. But these weren't the actual reasons for rejecting me. I knew the reason, but somehow my parents were in denial until they met Sonali.

Sonali worked as a Java developer with TCS in Gurgoan. Her profile picture spoke volumes about her beauty and confidence. She was ambitious and wished to continue with her job even after marriage. Her hobbies included watching reality shows on TV, playing with puppies – so much so that she wanted to have a pet puppy after marriage. She was unaware then that she'd get two puppies if she married me.

One fine Sunday, we visited her place to meet her. As usual, some boring and irrelevant topics were discussed. Her parents, being very smart, poked me twice so that I'd utter something. But I only nodded at whatever they asked. After half an hour of normal chatting, Sonali and I were blessed with some time in isolation.

The real struggle for me began then. A beautiful girl looks killer when she puts on make-up. She was looking like a queen, and I felt like a poor man. I went numb, not because of her beauty, but because of the isolation.

After smiling for around five minutes, Sonali asked, "Any questions for me, Vijay?"

"No," I replied hesitantly, "but if you have any, feel free to ask."

And the very next second, she began talking like a tape recorder. I realized that I had committed the cardinal sin.

"What are your future plans?"

"Where did you study?"

"Do you stay in a rented flat or own it?"

"How is your job?"

"Are you closer to your father or your mother?"

"Did you ever have any girlfriend?"

"Do you have any psychological problem?"

"Do you have any health related issues?"

"What is your salary?"

"Do you have any bad habits?"

I answered a few questions straightaway, but got irritated later. I am thankful that she didn't ask me the size of my dick.

"Haven't you gone through my profile? The answers to all these have already been mentioned there," I said.

There was a well-known silence in the room. She replied with a cunning smile, "I think we would be good as friends."

Well, that did not surprise me at all, but it also had Sonali's answer hidden in it. The very same evening, Sonali's mother called up and expressed her regret. "Vijay is a very nice boy, but Sonali is actually looking for a government employee. We are really very sorry."

This shot my mother's blood to boiling temperature and she shouted aloud on the phone, "This is disgusting! His profile was shared on the website. If your daughter had different demands, then we shouldn't have been invited in the first place."

I was sitting very close to my mother and could easily comprehend her conversation with Sonali's mother.

"My son has a heart of gold," said my mother. "I bet that you cannot find anyone better than him for your daughter." I looked at myself in the mirror and wondered whether my mother was actually talking about me.

Hearing my mother's words, Sonali couldn't hold back any longer. "Hi Aunty," she took the phone from her mother and rattled away.

My mother kept mum, but that didn't discourage Sonali. She further said, "Let me tell you the actual reason for my rejection. I am totally fine marrying a teacher or even an Asst. Prof. for that matter. But your son hardly speaks a word. He is an introvert and a boring person. He has below average looks and lacks confidence. If it is difficult for you to digest these facts, then please consider my former reason of denying him. Hope you have got your answers now. Goodbye and all the best for your great son's future." Saying all this in one breath, Sonali disconnected the call.

My mother could hardly bear that insult. In her boiling rage she said, "How dare she disconnect the call!" and dialled her number again. This time, however, I held her and said politely, "Mom, enough of running away from reality."

There was an abrupt silence and tears rolled down my mother's eyes. She is not a lady who gives up easily. She is egoistic. She shouted at my dad, "Sanjay, you are to be blamed for this!"

That was it. Now the two age old enemies were ready to spoil the rest of the happiness in my life.

"What the hell did I do?" Papa retaliated.

"You have always forced your dreams on him. You never asked him about his wishes and dreams. That sucked out all the confidence from him.I cannot accept an idiot like Sonali calling my son an introvert."

"Stop shifting the blame onto me. Let me remind you that I work for the police force and am out for majority of the time. You have spent the most important moments of your son's life with him."

"Is it? Was it me who wanted him to be an IAS officer? No! It was you. You wanted him to continue attempting for that stupid exam which wasted his five precious years!"

In spite of theirs being a love marriage, I couldn't spot even an ounce of love between them now. They rarely spoke to each other and whenever they did, the conversation would witness raised volumes, ending up in a quarrel. Thank god for our small two BHK apartment which had bound us to face each other, else none of us were even willing to look at the other's face.

●

"Vijay, please dress up. We are going out for lunch," my mother instructed me one fine morning while I was lazying around peacefully. My intelligent mind immediately decoded the intention behind this lunch – another girl-seeing program!

"She is the daughter of one of my old friends and knows everything about you."

I was left wondering what was covered in this *everything*. 'Is she aware that I am a hopeless man?' I wanted to ask. As we headed towards Mukherjee Nagar, I have no idea what crossed my mother's mind, but she started chanting her all-time instructions. "Vijay, please understand, my son. I know that as a person, you are the best human being. But every girl wants to marry a confident man."

"Okay."

"Please open up, son. Express yourself. A silent person is just like a closed box – people are unaware of the stuff hidden in it. Whereas an expressive person is just like an open book – howsoever much one tries, they cannot change the contents. It can be read by one and even by millions. Be like a book." Now here was a new definition of me – a closed box!

I nodded and no matter how much I wanted to say, 'I understand', I kept mum. But my mother understood my emotions. This was not the first time I was receiving this inspirational speech from my mother and I was well aware of ways to avoid it – silence.

We reached the destined place and my parents were welcomed. I settled in one corner of the sofa and scanned the room inquisitively. My mother immediately sprang into action by flaunting the most famous hero of Bollywood.

"My son is very obedient and brilliant. He has cleared his PCS entrance exam and one day he'll be an IPS officer just like his father. Although he isn't interested in his current job, he is just parking himself while preparing for a government job."

My father stared at me. He seemed happy that at least my mother was appreciating him in others' presence.

"Vijay has never even touched alcohol, let alone his having a girlfriend."

Isn't that the reason why we were here? Had I had a girlfriend, why would we have met these people? My weakness of being unable to have a girlfriend was somehow showcased as my strength. After a few minutes, my mother's next target, a lady entered the room. Speaking of her just as a lady would not be enough. She looked like a model with her shining hair, adorned in black and white Punjabi suit with high heeled sandals making her five feet six inches tall. On her ears glittered small diamond studs. She had a perfect body, with all the curves at the appropriate places. Her cheek bones made her look like Kareena Kapoor in size zero. After a few seconds, I was apprised that this model had just landed a job with Axis bank. The beautiful name of this beautiful girl was Astha.

Mr Vijay, be ready for another rejection! I made a mental note.

I had prepared myself for the worst. It is very interesting to know that once you are prepared for the worst, your confidence touches the sky, because you have absolutely nothing to lose. I glanced at Astha and our eyes met for the first time ever. She smiled, but I was too engrossed in her beauty to smile back at her. However, I wasn't nervous as I was already prepared for the worst.

"Astha, why don't you take him along to the nearby ice-cream shop?" her mother suggested. After almost a dozen bride-hunts, I was familiar with these formalities. For me, it was an opportunity to chat with a model. We were just about to move when my mother said, "Vijay, come soon." Her merciful eyes were pleading me to talk openly with Astha. I nodded.

Five minutes into our walk to the nearby ice-cream parlour, Astha took the first step to strike a conversation.

"Do you like ice-cream?"

"Occasionally."

We reached the parlour and settled at the extreme corner table. Being a Sunday afternoon, the place wasn't much crowded.

"Welcome to the ice-cream wonderland of New Zealand. We pioneer in natural ice cream flavours," a waiter said and asked Astha her choice. It amazed me to see how expert these waiters are to extract an order from ladies, offering maximum courtesy to them and conveniently ignoring the fact that the bill could be paid by the man too.

Astha was busy going through the menu while asking for my preferance.

"Nothing specific," I said as choice of ice cream was millions of miles away from my mind. I was busy looking at her. The way she spoke to the waiter, her hairstyle, the way her hands moved... everything mesmerized me. And as expected, I was playing my part of remaining silent and observing this beauty with brains.

"Vijay, why are you so silent?" she shot her first question. What would I have said? That this is how I am?

"Nothing like that, do you have a boyfriend?" I blurted out something I could never even imagine in my dreams. This is what happens when you force someone to speak.

"So, you want a virgin?" She instantly concluded. I was aghast with the frankness with which she said this.

"No, no, you totally misunderstood me." I tried covering up for my blunder. "I was only wondering how a girl like you doesn't have a boyfriend and how you opted for an arranged marriage. That's it."

She smiled, but chose not to reply. Meanwhile, we were served our ice-cream.

"You don't seem to have any particular inclination towards ice cream flavours, do you?" she asked. I was never aware that an ice cream would come to my rescue someday. I shook my head and Astha fired another question.

"Are you seriously preparing for the IPS?"

"No," was my first direct answer.

"Then what is your plan for the future, Vijay?"

"Nothing huge."

"Do you have any past?" This question was weird for a person who was not clear even about his present.

"I feel that is trivial."

"Hmm." She smiled and asked, "Do you eat non-veg?"

"No, I belong to an orthodox Brahmin family."

"Do you like drinking alcohol?"

"I have never even touched alcohol, let alone pass it down my throat. I have already mentioned this in my profile," I replied sounding a bit irritated. She was taken aback with the sudden change in my tone.

"But what if you future wife loves to booze?" My irritation had had no lasting effect on her.

"I appreciate personal freedom, but also believe that there has to be a limit to everything." I think that was the first time when I had answered someone with such maturity.

"What do you aspire to be?" I suddenly felt like I was being interviewed for the IAS.

"I only want to be a good human being." I couldn't have thought of a better answer; this made her smile.

"Vijay, do you have any specific questions for me?"

"Nothing much."

I was so sure that this model was going to reject me that I didn't even think of investing energy in speaking when I was sure that there would be no returns. At the same instant, I got a call from my mother. She was worried because she had wanted me to wind up my conversation with Astha soon. She knew that more interaction meant more chances of rejection.

"Vijay, I want to tell you about my past," she said, sounding serious. I was cent percent sure that she was about to reveal something that I didn't wish to hear.

"Vijay, the woman who was introduced to you as my mother is my stepmother. My father had an affair with my mom. When she passed away due to a heart attack, I ended up with this family," she said with difficulty. "I am an illegitimate child." Saying this, she went silent. I guessed that she was about to cry.

Throughout my life I had believed that I had trouble with my terrible parents, but her story seemed to carry more pain.

"Astha, no child is illegitimate. Don't ever say that. If anyone is illegitimate, then it's the parents, not their children." Hearing this, she heaved a sigh of relief.

"You are a nice man," she said.

She was feeling low and I thought of sharing something about myself to make her feel better. "Astha," I said, "I am not a professor, but an assistant professor who is only an ad hoc faculty. My father is a retired IPS officer. Ours is not a wealthy family. I was never good at studies. And to tell you something interesting, you are the fourteenth girl I am meeting."

Astha looked at me the way the rest of the thirteen girls had looked at me. She went quiet. After a few seconds, I suggested that we should leave. She nodded and we started walking; silence still prevailed. I think my revelation helped her make her decision. Before entering her house, Astha said something that I had heard before. "Vijay, I think we'd be good friends."

●

"How is Astha?"

My mother commenced her interrogation as soon we started for home. Her question amused me but being a shy person, it was easy for me to hide my blush. I was sure that I would have been the topper had this question been asked in the IAS exam. But to my mother, I just managed to say that she looked good. I didn't want to raise their hopes as I was anticipating a negative outcome of my meeting. I didn't even share the fact that she was an illegitimate child. A few more days passed without receiving any call from Astha's mother.

The answer was obvious, but not receiving a call was more heartbreaking for my mother than a rejection because Astha's mother was her colleague too. My mother again started her endless inspirational speech for me to speak up. I was now convinced that another rejection from a girl would result in me landing up in speech therapy sessions. A few days later, we received the news that Astha's father had passed away due to brain hemorrhage. I pitied Astha. She had lost her mother during her childhood and now she had lost her father too. I wondered how a girl who looks so charismatic and confident could have such a painful life. I felt an urge to call her but I, Vijay Sharma, once again, saved my energy by keeping silent.

After a span of about two weeks, my mother had a reason to smile. Astha had agreed for our alliance! My family was exhilarated. I had a serious doubt about her answer and so I approached my dad, "Why is she marrying me??"

My father smiled at me and said, "This is the same question I had asked myself when your mother had said yes."

"But yours was a love marriage!" I countered him.

"Love can happen after marriage too."

His answer failed to satisfy me and till date, the same question continues to poke me – why did she marry me? Anyway, I was neither interested in love, nor lust. For me, I had cleared my IAS exam when Astha accepted me as the man of her life.

Our wedding date was about to be fixed when Astha called me up one day. "Vijay, please tell your parents about my past. I don't want to hide anything."

Taking her cue, I informed papa about her being born out of an illegitimate affair. My father's response made me proud of him. He said, "These things hardly matter. Astha is a nice girl. However, please refrain from discussing this with your mother."

'Astha weds Vijay' read a board on the day of the wedding. But, for me, it read: 'Extrovert weds Introvert', 'Celebrity weds Commoner', 'Winner weds Loser'.

3

Finally, I was a married man. I had gotten an ounce of happiness after a really long time. Astha and I were two very different personalities. I got a beautiful and lovable wife who had all the qualities to qualify her as being a celebrity's wife. But as a price of having her in my life, I ended up losing my home.

Astha loved non-vegetarian food and drinks. She loved to party and I hated it, both for the same reason – people and gatherings. I preferred to live alone. Every now and then she would force me to have a drink with her, but I managed to refrain. I never stopped her from doing anything. I appreciated personal space and being bossy was not my style. She was eating non-vegetarian food in a Brahmin family who hated even the slightest smell of it. After one month of our marriage, I got the first puncture in my happiness balloon when my mother got to know about Astha being an illegitimate child. My mother behaved with her as if she were a whore. Astha, however, was not the kind who would gulp down all the poison and remain silent. She blurted out, "I had cleared everything with my husband during our pre-marriage meet."

To not get burnt from the fire in which my mother was already burning, I diverted the flames towards Papa, saying, "Mom, I had apprised Papa about this and he suggested that I keep it from you."

Now the age old enemies had one more reason to fight. After the revelation about Astha, my mother began to hold her responsible for everything. Our home had turned into a battlefield. Every now and then, my mother and Astha would fight over trivial issues.

After almost four months of an incessant tug of war, the rope finally broke when my mother stumbled upon the bottle cap of a breezer. She darted a direct question at all of us, "Who was drinking in my house?"

No one answered, but everyone knew that it was Astha. The last nail in the coffin was when my mother sniffed that Astha had cooked omelet at home in her absence. In a Brahmin household where no one had ever tasted meat, a person who eats non-vegetarian food and drinks alcohol is termed as a sinner. How could Astha behave in this fashion? I question myself about my actions while all this was happening right under my nose and as usual, I remained silent.

A couple of times my mother declared me as a henpecked husband. I couldn't understand what that meant, but one thing that I knew for sure was that whenever my mother said that I was henpecked, it only meant that she had surrendered in the great battle between mother-in-law and daughter-in-law.

After five months of battle, Astha finally won. As a result, it was decided that we would move to a separate rented flat in Malviya Nagar, close to her workplace. This being the official reason of our shift, there were multitude unofficial reasons.

I gradually made it a trend to visit my parents' place every Saturday because Saturday would be an off for me and a day in office for Mom and Astha.

Isolating Mom and Astha had given me a few days of peace. Neither did my wife complain about my mother, nor vice versa. I was finally away from all the nagging business. Everything seemed to be perfect – a beautiful wife, dual working members, no nagging at home, and happiness. But life had again managed to prove that Mr Vijay had to suffer till the very end.

My only reason of happiness, my wife, had been diagnosed positive with HIV.

I couldn't believe it. I wondered if I was watching a movie. Was all of this actually happening with me? How did she get infected? Was she having an affair? Was I infected with HIV too? Will my wife die? All these questions deluged my mind. There was absolute silence in the room. It was the deepest and darkest silence of my life.

Whatever little knowledge I had about the disease comprised that AIDS was incurable and my wife was certainly going to die.

Imagining these scenes which I had only seen in movies froze me to the core. Human brain is the most beautiful yet the most dangerous creation which can make us realize the reality. I sprinted straight towards my wardrobe, a section of which was being used as a temple, and where a dozen idols were kept. I folded my hands and said, "I cannot accept this. Why am I always the target? Don't you have anyone else in your list to torture? Why is it me every single time? Why God, why? If you exist, please help me!"

4

I switched my laptop on. For the next couple of minutes, my keywords in the search engine were: How do we get AIDS? Available cure for HIV? Specialist doctor near Malviya Nagar, New Delhi? Sex and AIDS?

Q. If a person becomes infected with HIV, does that mean he has AIDS?
No, HIV is an unusual virus. A person can be infected with it for many years and yet appear to be perfectly healthy. But the virus gradually multiplies inside the body and eventually destroys the body's ability to fight off illnesses.

It is still not certain whether everyone with HIV infection will get AIDS. It seems likely that most people with HIV will develop serious health problems, but this could take several years. A person with HIV may not know he is infected, but can pass the virus on to other people.

Q. How long does it take for HIV to cause AIDS?
Since 1992, scientists have estimated that about half the people with HIV develop AIDS within ten years of getting infected. This time varies greatly from person to person and can depend on many factors, including a person's health status and their health-related behaviours.

Today there are medical treatments that can slow down the rate at which HIV weakens the immune system. Early detection offers more options for treatment and preventative healthcare.

Q. Why do people who are infected with HIV eventually die?
When people are infected with HIV, they do not die of HIV or AIDS. They die due to the effects that HIV has on the body. With the immune system down, the body becomes susceptible to many infections, from the common cold to deadly diseases like cancer. It is actually those particular infections, and the body's inability to fight the infections, that causes death.

Q. Tests for HIV and AIDS
Blood tests are the most common way to diagnose the Human Immunodeficiency Virus (HIV), the virus that causes Acquired Immuno Deficiency Syndrome (AIDS).

It can take from six weeks to six months to develop antibodies to the virus, and follow-up tests may be needed. Your doctor will ask about your symptoms, medical history and risk factors and perform a physical examination.

The primary tests for diagnosing HIV and AIDS include:

- **ELISA Test** – Enzyme-Linked Immunosorbent Assay – is used to detect HIV infection. If an ELISA test is positive, the Western blot test is usually administered to confirm the diagnosis. If an ELISA test is negative, but you think you may have HIV, you should be tested again in one to three months.

  ELISA is quite sensitive in a chronic HIV infection, but because antibodies aren't produced immediately upon infection, you may test negative in the first few months after being infected. Even though your test result may be negative during this window, you may have a high level of the virus and be at the risk of transmitting infection.

- **Western Blot** – This is a very sensitive blood test used to confirm a positive ELISA test result.

When I was in the middle of my research, my phone rang.

"Hi Sharmaji, whats up?"

"Nothing. Just missing my wife."

"Really?"

"Obiously."

"Your wife is leaving for home. Do you want to have some hot samosas? Or maybe a drink?" she said with a hint of naughtiness in her voice.

"No no, you know I don't drink. Just come home, I have something special for you."

"Surprise? Okay. I'll be leaving in fifteen minutes."

I called Dr Lal PathLabs after the chat and scheduled my timings for the sample collection for the next morning. The lady who was talking on the other side enquired about the tests I wanted to undergo.

"ELISA and Western blot for two adults."

"Please wait a minute," she said and put me on hold. After a moment of silence, she asked in an unsure voice, "This is for HIV, sir?"

●

My doorbell rang and the most beautiful woman in my life entered with a bang.

"Good evening, dear," Astha barged in cheerfully. Her entry always filled the house with life. I was worried about the impact of her infection now, if at all it was really there.

"Good evening, darling." We hugged and kissed.

"I am hungry," she said and went straight to the kitchen.

She was a real foodie and in the short period of six months, I had realized that she wanted something to eat immediately after reaching home. She never changed or even washed her hands or feet. When she was hungry, then nothing could stand in between food and her tummy.

"Wait, I have a surprise for you!" I said and walked in before her.

She frowned. I went to the kitchen and brought what I had made. It was not her favourite dish, but she had not had one for a while.

"An omelette! You made an omelette for me. Am I dreaming?" she took a bite. "You never liked this, you hated the smell. I am so surprised…how come a true vegetarian is doing this! Your mother will get a heart attack if she comes to know!" she always asked question and answered them herself. Actually, she was slightly talkative, but I don't want to say that.

"Why do *you* need to compromise all the time?" was all I managed to say even though I was flooded with emotions.

"Is this the Vijay of Malviya Nagar or Vijay Dinanath Chauhan from *Agnipath*?" she mocked imitating Amitabh Bachan's voice. I smiled.

"Vijay, allow me to have one more of my favourite things," she said and went inside the kitchen. I knew her love for vodka. She came out with two glasses, some vodka and orange juice.

"Vijay, let's celebrate the day." In spite of knowing that I don't drink, she poured out two glasses. She often behaved weirdly.

"What is the reason for this celebration?"

"I am meeting my husband after twenty days. Is it not enough reason to celebrate?"

"You want excuses to drink," I said. She smiled mischievously.

"C'mon, cheers!" She lifted her glass. Her euphoria did not last long.

"You know I don't drink."

"I wonder why! It's colourless and mixed with juice. I thought you might have tried some in Goa," she said in disappointment.

"But don't you worry, celebrations will continue. I will join you with fruit juice."

"Vijay, just try at least. We are not committing any sin."

"I know. And I will try some other day. I am in no mood to try anything today." She pouted and made a sad face as I said this.

"Astha, one day I will drink for you, but not today." I was not orthodox, and definitely not one to believe drinking to be sin. I was just scared because I had never tried. If I had one, she would have forced me to have the next and I was not sure what I would blurt out. She avoided my futile excuses and jumped on the omelette.

Her slurping tongue, chewing sound and delighted eyes were saying more than her words. I was happy to have given her that moment of happiness.

"Don't stare like that," she came close and whispered. "See Sharmaji, I am the winner."

"How?"

"Once you stopped me from having an omelette at home and remember what I said, 'One day you will yourself make an omelette for me.' See, you did."

I passed a smile. She emptied her glass and I had the juice, sip by sip.

"Now I am sure, one day, you will serve a drink for me too," she smiled and said.

I was speechless, but her happiness was piercing me. I decided I would not reveal to her the news about HIV till it was confirmed. Maybe after that too. I was a helpless husband who wanted her time to be spent happily. I said with utmost love, "You will always remain a winner."

5

After dinner, we snuggled in bed while having a light chat. The zero watt red light bulb was creating the perfect ambience. In spite of my inner turmoil, there was an aura of happiness in the room. It was one of the loveliest moments of my life, not because it was the first time that we were snuggling, but because my perception of things had begun to change. After three weeks of separation, my physical urges were at a high. I could even decode her whispers, but the irony was that I could not make love to an HIV patient.

"So, what did you do the whole day?" she asked while getting closer to me. Our nostrils were so close that we could easily inhale each other's breath.

"I went to a doctor." Even before I could finish what I had to say, she cut me short.

"Doctor? Are you okay?"

"Well, some problem. It hurts while peeing," I said hesitatingly.

"Hurts? Where? Don't tell me it's in the penis?"

"Yeah," I said with a sad face, contorted with pain.

"What the hell! After a trip to Goa, my husband's penis is hurting!" She frowned and stared at me with suspicion. "I hope you didn't sleep with anyone."

"Shut up!" When we speak the truth, raising our voice in protest is trivial. Even a gentle shut-up is enough. "I might have masturbated thinking of you, though. Ever thought I could have missed you that much! Why do you always have to think negative?" I responded bitterly while she giggled.

"Sorry, I was just joking. What did the doctor say?"

"She said I have a urinary tract infection, because of which I'll have to avoid having sex for a couple of days," I said, carefully making the doctor a female to tease her.

"You went to a woman to get yourself examined?! Oh my god, my husband and a doctor! Noooo!" she went on acting up, over dramatizing her expressions like a cheesy South Indian movie. Then she stiffened up a bit, as if remembering something. "What did you just say? No sex for a couple of days?" she repeated, despair clearly resonating in her voice.

She was just about to say something when I kissed her and said, "Allow me to finish. Today I have activated an insurance policy of ten lakhs, which is subject to medical tests for both of us. So tomorrow, an assistant from Dr Lal PathLabs will be coming over to collect a sample." I sighed.

She nodded and I added another instruction, "You have to have an empty stomach until the blood sample is collected, which will approximately be done around eight in the morning."

She went silent. In order to change the topic, I asked, "When is your job confirmation due?"

"Monday."

"How is your manager?" I continued to try making her talk so as to divert her attention from the infected penis.

"That idiot Mukul Mathur!" she almost screamed.

"Did he do anything that troubled my darling?"

"The bank's official closing time is five and I leave at half past five. Even then he accuses me of leaving office early!" she looked at me hoping for me to support her. A husband has to have her wife's back, so I shook my head and clicked my tongue in support.

"Why does he compare his life with mine?" she continued. "He is buried in his desk until eight. How am I at fault for that?" She was up with her one-sided conversation. "He earns in lakhs; he can sit in office twenty-four hours. But you know what, he is the worst boss."

"Absolutely!" I smiled and said, "Why don't you quit, sweetheart?"

"You are right. I should switch my job."

"No, I am not asking you to switch. I suggest that you leave this boring banker job and pursue your dream."

"Well, let me tell you about an incident that'll make you laugh. Sargam and I would always chat about our aspirations in life, and co-incidentally, we both wanted to be actresses."

"Really? You wanted to be an actress?" I smiled at her and asked inquisitively.

"Please don't laugh." I usually smile at everything and very rarely do I laugh, whereas she is completely the opposite. That's why she considered my smile as laugh.

"Once I felt I wanted to be a writer. Can you believe it? Astha Pathak, a writer!"

I freed her from my arms and looked at her intently to show my interest. "Why not? I am sure you must have written a few pages too!"

"Yes, I did write some pages."

"Where are those pages? How have you not shown them to me yet? And yes, now I am absolutely sure that you should quit your job and pursue writing."

"Professor Sharma ji, fifteen thousand house rent plus ten thousand for other expenses per month and your salary is twenty-five thousand. What if we want to buy a new car or something else? How will we be able to manage the money for it? At the end of the day, we'll be left with nothing."

"Just think, once you become a writer, millions of each of your books will be sold and then I'll ask you the same question. Then your answer will change."

"But how can you be so sure that each book of mine will sell a million copies."

"I am very positive about that. Just show me the pages that you had written." I sat up with excitement and said, "Show me your manuscript!"

I didn't want my wife to be working while struggling to fight against HIV. However, the diagnosis had to be confirmed first.

"I can smell a rat! Are you up to something? Whatever you say, I am not going to resign."

"Astha, look at yourself. You return home frustrated. It is only a matter of time before your frustration becomes permanent. Try to pursue your dream instead." I tried convincing her for the first time ever.

"I am not quitting and the discussion is over." She authoritatively put an end to our discussion.

"At least show me what you wrote, Astha."

"When I was done writing, I realized that I couldn't be a writer. It's not worth reading."

"It hardly matters what you think. Just show me the pages," I said, but she didn't move an inch.

"Okay, don't show me all the pages. How many did you write?" I forced her.

She looked at me with merciful eyes and took a deep breath before saying, "One."

6

Next morning, an assistant from Dr Lal PathLabs arrived to collect our samples. Astha shared her blood sample without an ounce of suspicion. As an exception, I requested them to deliver the report on priority. Before leaving, he shared the most important instruction while handing over a pamphlet to me: "If there are any extreme discoveries, you'll receive a call from the lab."

Astha was getting ready to leave for office. I copied a few numbers from her cell phone while she had gone for a shower. That day, I dropped her to the office. I had decided not to let her carry on with her job, but I couldn't find the right words to convince her. I had to come up with a couple of good reasons to convince her. Since my college was closed for the next one month, I had only one thing on priority – to fix everything before resuming college.

Around one in the afternoon, while I was resting, I realized that before anything else, I had to confirm whether I too was HIV positive. Just then, I received a call from an unknown landline number. I picked it up with a lot a fear and anticipation.

"Hello, we are calling Dr Lal PathLabs. Am I talking to—"

I cut her short and asked fearfully, "I am Vijay. Are the reports ready? What is the outcome?"

I had said all this at lightning speed. My heart was beating faster with every passing second.

"Sir, your HIV report is negative," answered the lady on the other side of the call.

"And what about Astha Sharma?" I asked. She sighed and paused. I guessed that she didn't have good news to share. "Please say it."

"Sir, you can download the reports from our website in an hour's time. All the details have been mentioned in the report."

"Please answer whether her report is positive or negative." Her delayed response had been killing me.

"Mrs Astha Sharma has been diagnosed positive for HIV. Her CD4 count is around 320cells/mm^3."

I abruptly disconnected the call without even caring to exchange formalities with the caller. It was a complex situation. I closed my eyes and a stream of tears rolled down my cheeks. For the first time in my life, I was feeling so helpless.

My entire life flashed in front of me. I sat in one corner of the room and sobbed.

●

I booted my laptop and began searching for information related to AIDS. Almost as a reflex, my fingers typed in these keywords – best doctor for HIV / AIDS in Delhi.

I found Dr Raza, HOD, Internal Medicine, at Max Hospital near Select City Walk, a kilometre away from my home. Thirty minutes later, I was standing outside his cabin, waiting to see him. I requested her assistant for the last appointment and received a suspicious look from her for making such an unusual request.

She said, "We do not work that way. If you want to consult him at the end, you might as well wait till the end. He'll be here till four o'clock only."

I wanted to be the last one to consult him so that he could spend a decent amount of time with me. There were several tasks to be accomplished. First and foremost, I had to apprise my family about the disease. Then I had to choose a suitable hospital, fix her career, and the most important of all, reveal the truth to her. How would she react? How would my parents react? A web of thoughts was hitting my nerves. I had never before applied my mind to anything in such detail.

After waiting for two hours, I finally got the chance to have a word with the doctor.

"Good afternoon sir," I greeted him as soon as I entered the room.

Inside the room, I found a middle-aged bespectacled man, slightly bald, with an air of confidence about him. His white coat indicated that he was indeed the senior doctor. He was clearing his desk and I, of course, was the last patient.

"Hi, the patient's name is Astha..." he looked at me doubtfully and guessed correctly that I wasn't the patient.

"She is not here. I am her husband, Vijay."

"Oh okay. Tell me," he said in a hurry, wishing to wind up for the day as soon as possible.

"Sir, this is her report," I said while placing a print out on his table. Along with her report, I showed him mine too.

It's good that doctors do not speak to the patient while going through the reports. He flipped a few pages of the report without paying any heed to what I was saying, focussing on the CD4 count. He was assured about the disease. He remained calm which indicated that he was not seeing such a report for the first time.

"Sir," I said getting emotional, "I got to know about this today. Is there any cure available in any part of the world?"

"I'm so sorry," he said with sensitivity. "I can understand your concern, but until now, medical science has been unable to find a cure for this. Over many years of research, doctors have understood many things. For example, we can control the duration for HIV to turn into AIDS. We can get some extra years of hope and life, provided all necessary medication starts at the earliest."

"Do you mean to say that it is curable?"

"Not completely. If the patient is medicated appropriately, with all the necessary care given to her, then the patient can live for many years."

"How many years, doctor?"

"We cannot quantify it, Mr Vijay Remember, an AIDS patient doesn't die because of AIDS. It only reduces their immunity, making home for other diseases which proves fatal. They can't even fight a common cold. But we can control the rate at which HIV turns into AIDS."

"Doctor, I need a personal favour from you. I hope you'll understand."

He nodded.

"My wife is unaware that she is HIV positive and I lack the courage to tell her about it. The moment she gets to know about it, the world will change for her. Her smiling face will be smiling no more. Along with crying and scolding me from the corner of the room, I want her to spend the rest of her time smiling."

"I can understand. What can I do for you?"

"Doctor, can I expect all support, care and medicine without informing her of the disease?"

"How can that be possible?" he said looking at me. "This disease requires a lot of care and precautions, and only an aware person can take better care of themselves. And what am I supposed to tell her when she is here? Don't ask me to treat her remotely. I cannot extend my treatment without meeting the patient."

"I will bring her here, but you only have to say that she is suffering from some disease that needs all the necessary care."

The doctor thought for a while and said, "My profession doesn't allow me to mislead the patients. I can hide information, but cannot lie. In fact, I would suggest that you too avoid lying to her." I absorbed his words and her teary face flashed in front of my eyes. A husband who didn't want to tell her wife that she has limited time to live had broken down.

"Be brave dear," pacified the doctor and offered me a glass of water. I ignored the water and asked where the washroom was. He showed me the way.

Inside the washroom, I cried silently, because for the first time, I was facing the heat of the reality from a doctor who was not ready to help me. I washed my face, cleared my throat, looked at my shabby face in the mirror and decided to face him.

The doctor who had seemed to be in a rush a few minutes back was now looking worried and at ease.

"Listen Vijay, you can do one thing," he said. "Just tell her that she is suffering from liver cirrhosis and it requires exhaustive care. Tomorrow I'll be leaving for an AIDS conference and will be back in three days. I'll prescribe VIRADAY medicine for the next three days. Give her these and get her here on the fourth day. I'll conduct all the necessary tests here itself. And you need not worry because I'll not tell her that she is suffering from HIV. I will also avoid writing anything related to HIV on the prescription."

His words overwhelmed me. "Thank you so much, doctor. Can you also suggest three months of bed rest in the prescription?"

"I will." He nodded. "Ask her to drink more water. If she is working somewhere, then the nature of her job should not be stressful. Avoid anything that can lead her to catch an infection of any sort. If you have a car, start using it to help her commute. Avoid letting her use a bike or public transport. You have to take care of her like a child."

"Thank you so much, sir." He nodded in acknowledgement and I got up to leave.

"Wait Vijay," he said just when I was about to open the door. He drank a glass of water and seemed to be moved. I sensed that he was sentimental. "I have been treating HIV patients since a decade. But no one in a situation similar to yours has approached me. Every HIV infected patient has approached me with a certain prejudice. They usually ask about the source of this infection. Some of them even ask me whether the patient had been involved in sex activities. They always come with a doubt about the patient's character. What they don't know is that apart from sex, there are various other sources of this infection. But for the first time I have met a person like you who has a different concern altogether."

"Appreciate your point, doctor. But just for curiosty's sake, is there a chance to diagnose the source of the infection?"

"No Vijay, we know the probable reasons that can cause infection, but no one can identify the source."

I nodded and remained silent.

He seemed to be expecting a few words in return, but in my current state of mind, I could only manage to pass a smile. He gave his last official instruction of the day saying, "Take care of your wife. You are a nice husband, Vijay. And use a condom."

I returned home at around five in the evening and still had more than an hour at hand to think in peace. I was wondering why the doctor had said his last words about me being a nice husband. I was not habituated to hearing such kind words about myself. Or maybe I had to prove that I was indeed a good husband. I didn't know what I was.

I had known Astha for the past six months. These six months were enough for me to understand her as a person. I was sure that a twenty-seven-year-old woman must definitely be having some hidden desires which she had never shared with her husband. She could have told someone very close to her, after her husband, of course. Only one such person's name came to my mind. Astha often spoke about her and I had her number as well. But would she not inform Astha about my call? Shall I hide the truth from her? How would she react?

7

Sargam Speaks

*H*i *friends. Though I am not a writer, I am here for my best friend, Astha.*

I vividly remember the day Vijay called me up. It was strange to see his name flash on my mobile screen because he had never called me earlier. I knew almost everything about him from Astha, but we had not communicated directly. A call from him meant that something serious had happened and from the way he spoke, I was nothing less than scared.

He asked me a few very weird questions. He asked me about Astha's desires and wishes. I was taken aback and countered him for an explanation. Vijay is bad at keeping things from people and upon insistence, he revealed to me the worst news possible – my friend was suffering from a rare kind of blood infection and had limited time to live. I was not told the name of the disease, but was sure that it was very serious. I couldn't gauge the gravity of his questions earlier, but with this fact known, I was unable to answer them and disconnected the call thinking about Astha.

We had studied together after our fifth standard. Astha had had a terrible childhood. While all the kids were enjoying their sapid lunches, her menu for lunch was fixed – it would always be either bread with jam or sandwiches. She had amazing potential. She would always come second or third in the school. I had made a deliberate attempt to befriend her by offering her my tiffin. With time, we became great friends who shared everything with each other.

Our story was like that of a flop movie. I had lost my parents in a car accident and found a saviour in my maternal uncle. He brought me up and cared for me like I was his own daughter. But an additional member in the family meant additional liability for them. When I met Astha, I realized that her life was more terrible than mine. Two people with similar stories always make good friends.

She had revealed her story to me about her fixed lunch menu. She had a stepmother. Her biological mother stayed alone and was occasionally visited by her father till Astha was in the fifth standard, after which she died. Her father brought her to a new place giving her an unwelcome chance of meeting her new mother. She had a loving father till the eight standard. One fine day, she got to know that her biological mother had never been married to her visitor father and she realized that she was an illegitimate child.

Astha's stepmother strengthened Astha's need for a good friend. We were both starving for motherly love and that strengthened our bond. Her stepmother was blessed with a baby, and Astha could sense the difference in her behaviour. She got her first shock when her mother slapped her for exchanging her tiffin with her younger sister. She realized that she was an unwanted guest in the house. That was the day when she declared herself an orphan.

Astha was a revengeful girl. If anyone betrayed her, she would never forgive that person. She would always want to defeat her enemy and never wanted anyone to sympathize with her. Every year, her younger sister's birthday would be celebrated like a carnival, whereas her birthday was celebrated only amongst us. She promised herself that she would become the best mother in the world. It was weird to even dream of it at that age, but sometimes our ego gives us a confidence boost.

Life was not that bad after she found love in Daniel, the topper of our college. Astha's dream to be a rich and famous person was going to be executed well with Daniel because he always adorned Astha with expensive gifts. He had even sponsored her last year's college fees.

Both of them graduated together from St. Stephen's College. Though I was not with her during the course of our graduation, I stayed close to her. The proximity of our houses had always made us frequent visitors at the other's place. We would party hard, eat non-vegetarian food and drink alcohol too.

Astha was a slight narcissist. She always wanted to become a celebrity and even marry a superstar – Salman Khan, to be specific. She was a crazy fan of his. She would always imagine her picture with Salman Khan on the front cover of a magazine. It is weird to admit but I too dreamt of the same, but with Shahrukh Khan. We would always have a fight over the superiority of Shahrukh over Salman or vice versa. She wanted to become a model and wished that a movie be made on her life. She wanted to own a Mercedes. We always dreamt big.

Her stepmother always cribbed about money. That was probably the reason for her dreaming to become rich. After graduation, when Astha once asked for money from her father, her mother protested, "Please try to understand that we have two liabilities and you are about to retire." That was the day when Astha decided not to ask for a single penny henceforth from her family.

In spite of being her best buddy, I had always hated her for being a snob. She was a girl who would prefer to die rather than ask for help. Her snobbish nature could only be handled by her boyfriend Daniel, who was another narcissist soul. After graduation, Daniel wished to study further. He cleared the entrance examination and his good score provided for a scholarship for him to pursue a two-year course with limited resources in the US. A day before his scheduled flight, he had come over to my house along with Astha. They had cried many times and I was sure that they must have vowed to each other to be together always. She was really sad that he would be leaving the next day. A girl who is not loved at home understands the importance of a friend. And when you have only one best friend, your boyfriend is a very crucial person in your life.

Daniel flew to the US and meanwhile, Astha cleared her PO examination at Axis Bank. She celebrated her success – as her motive was to tease her stepmother and stepsister. But happiness and Astha could not stay together for long. One day Daniel requested Astha to extend her help by issuing a personal loan to his father; it was an amount of two lakh rupees for his mother's treatment, since Daniel's father was not earning enough to bear the expenses of a foreign education along with treating his ill spouse. That day, life changed for Daniel and Astha.

I am not sure of what went wrong at Daniel's place, but Daniel's father met Astha and requested her to break all relations with Daniel. His family's Catholic beliefs and anti-Hindu mindset were the biggest hindrances to their union. The only blossom of her life slipped away right in front of her eyes and she couldn't do anything about it.

Astha visited my house and drank to her destiny. A couple of vodka shots later, in the moment of extreme disappointment, Astha made up her mind to break up with Daniel. It was then that I asked Astha to create a bucket-list of all her wishes that she wanted to fulfil before leaving this world. I did the same and right in front of her, but I wonder why she concealed her list from me. It was quite unlike Astha to hide things from me. It only meant that her bucket-list contained something grave.

Then came a marriage proposal from Vijay's family. Astha's stepmother worked with Vijay's mother and they were good friends. At first, Astha rejected the proposal because she found the guy average looking and an introvert. After a few days, Astha's only living biological parent, her father, had a brain hemorrhage and passed away. Astha lost everything she could call her own. She realized that Vijay was a nice person; a journalist mother and an inspector father made him a good human being; he was a budding PCS aspirant too. She agreed to the alliance without even informing Daniel about it.

In the meantime, Daniel was incessantly trying to reach Astha. She had changed her contact number and had cut off her past.

Post marriage, Astha realized that Vijay was a failure. He worked at the Sri Ram College of Arts, Science and Commerce as an assistant professor of English. She had ended up marrying only a teacher – a poor teacher at that. He never uttered a word against his mother who had issues with everything concerning Astha. She was trying to snatch away Astha's freedom and that was something that Astha couldn't tolerate. After five months of their marriage, both of them finally decided to move out of the house. She wanted to celebrate with me, and for Astha, celebration was a synonym for vodka.

Although Vijay had multiple shortcomings, the best thing about him was that he loved Astha from the core of his heart. She was done cribbing about the small things and had begun adjusting with reality – something that was not like my Astha.

Marriage always changes people and Astha had begun to change.

8

When I was done talking to Sargam, I started off to pick up my darling from her office. It was an unusual thing for me to do because our office timings almost always clashed. That's why I had never picked her up. But as suggested by the doctor, I wanted to ensure her comfort.

On our way home, I enquired about her boss, "So, is Mr Mukul Mathur still in office?"

"The fucking Mathur will die in the bank," she replied in frustration, "he doesn't have anything else to do in life!"

I would never use the word 'fuck', not even at night, but it was embedded in her vocabulary. I dropped her home and lied, "I'll be home in an hour's time. I have to go to the insurance office. They have called me for a discussion about my policy and health reports."

"The same reports for which we had given our samples today morning?" she asked. I nodded and went off.

I stopped right in front of the bank. There was an ATM kiosk. I was right in the middle of a crowded market and at seven in the evening in Delhi, it is easier to locate an ATM than a parking space.

The ATM guard stopped me in my way saying, "Sir, the bank is closed and you cannot go inside."

"I am here to see Mr Mukul. Please inform him that Astha Sharma's husband wants to have a word with him."

"Oh, you are a staff's relative! I thought you're a customer. Sorry for stopping you. You may go inside, please." I was certain that Astha's kind personality never went unnoticed, not even by the guard.

There was pin drop silence in the bank. I turned my neck to find a cabin at one corner of the hallway. This must be the devil's abode, I thought. I was impressed with the man's commitment to his job. His cabin door was ajar, and I peeped inside the cabin. Our eyes met for a moment and he reacted unpleasantly. He quickly began to hide something under the table.

"May I come in, sir?" I requested.

"The bank is closed. How did you manage to step inside?"

"Sir, I am Vijay Sharma. Astha's husband," I replied at the cabin's door.

"Oh, come in please," he said heaving a sigh of relief.

"It is perfectly fine, sir."

"Astha had left for the day at her usual time. Has she not reached home yet?"

"Sir, I am here to meet you. Astha is at home."

"Oh okay. What would you like to have? Tea or coffee?" his words contradicted with Astha's description of him as an inhuman being.

"You need not be so formal with me, sir."

"Please call me Mukul. Do you drink?" he asked playfully.

"No," I replied.

"Good," he said, placing a glass on the table followed by some snacks and finally a half-filled bottle of Royal Stag. I was offered a transparent, four inch glass.

"Sir, I don't drink," I repeated myself because he clearly hadn't understood my previous denial.

"It is just soft drink," he said pouring some Pepsi. "I am fed up of drinking alone."

"Thank you, sir. I salute your commitment as you are working post office hours. Every professional must learn from you." I was trying my hands at an art alien to me – the art of buttering.

"Call me Mukul, please," he said, emptying his glass in seconds. "Actually, the reason for my stay is personal. I stay here because I am not happy being at home. I have a terrible life. People think that I work a lot, whereas in reality, I am only running away from my daily mess."

It was unbelievable for me that a person was so frank with me about his family issues. I was confused. Was he the same boss who made my darling's life miserable each day or was it just the Royal Stag effect taking over his senses. I could easily see his swinging eyes and momentary happiness. I gussed he had attained inner peace.

"Oh, sorry to hear that," I said taking a sip of my drink.

"It's okay. I always wonder why people like us get married," he continued.

"The best part of it is that we get a loving person to share our entire life with," I said and smiled.

"Love and marriage can never go hand in hand. Oh, I am so sorry! I'm digressing. What made you come here?"

"Sir, I need your help and I am sure that understanding and loving that you are, you'll surely help me out," I buttered him some more before coming to the point.

He frowned at my words but said, "Feel free," while pouring another peg.

"Sir, Astha's promotion is due for Monday."

"Don't worry about that. I have already cleared her file and she will soon be a permanent employee of this bank."

He seemed to be uncontrollable. Had I asked for a loan of a hundred crore rupees, I am sure he would have sanctioned it without any second thoughts. That was the beauty of Royal Stag; it was making him behave royally.

"That, sir, is exactly the reason of my worry. Our doctor has suggested that she needs complete bed-rest as she is suffering from a fatal disease that—" I sighed before I could continue. It was difficult for me to speak. I could only manage to say, "She has only a few months to live."

"What! Are you serious?" he asked inquisitively while making another peg. There was silence in the room which I broke.

"Sir, she is not aware of the criticality of the disease. With my current financial condition, I cannot coax her to quit her job. I want to take care of her and prevent her from falling prey to any unnecessary infections. I want you to terminate her services after her probation because you wouldn't have to justify it to anyone."

He took a sip, thinking for a few seconds. "Vijay," he said, "If I terminate her without providing a valid reason for the same, it will shatter her confidence. Plus, this is against the HR policy as well. I am afraid I cannot do this. I definitely require a valid reason to do that. Also, what is the proof of your statement?"

"Sir, she will have to quit her job anyway. If you do not help me out, I'll be bound to reveal the truth to her, which would cause more pain than being terminated from her job." Saying this, I showed him the doctor's prescription which he took a look at in his half-conscious state of mind. He managed to understand the three month bed-rest part. I narrated my fake story of an insurance policy and medical test, at the end of which I finally added the truth. "Mukul sir," I said, "the moment she gets to know that she is suffering from a severe disease, she will not be the same happy-go-lucky Astha anymore."

"So, you are going to keep everything under wraps and try to make her happy for the rest of her time, is it?"

I nodded. I was impressed with the way his mind was working faster with every peg.

"Vijay, let me tell you something about Astha. She has been working here for the last two years. She had been regular with her time, but after her marriage, she would leave at around five and that would often upset me. But for the last few days, she has been staying back. I enquired about this change in her schedule from her colleague. It turned out that she would stay back in office because you were away for your college trip. I have always blamed her for not staying back in the evening and felt she was a disastrous professional. However, I believe that she is an extremely lucky person when it comes to her personal life."

"Thanks for your kind words, sir." I sighed. "So can I be assured that you'd be firing her?"

"Let me have a word with the HR."

"Sir, you are a very nice man. You could be a tough boss, but I know that you're a good person at heart. I believe you should spend some more time with your family rather than spending time at office and drinking in isolation. That way, you would be able to control your alcohol intake." I have no idea how or why I philosophized, maybe the words were coming straight from my heart.

"Thanks," he said and nodded, "but how do you know that I am a good person at heart?"

I smiled at him sadly and said, "Because you are going to fire her."

9

After returning from her office, I heaved a sigh of relief. That night in bed, I was thinking that a newly-wed couple often spent quality time together before dozing off; most of the times for one of the two reasons – working hard or talking. Unfortunately, I could not work hard with my wife for now, so we had to talk.

"Hey Astha," I said cuddling her, "I want to discuss something with you." Her head was resting over my left hand, hair tied by a clutch, and a night bulb waiting for the night show.

"Discussion and you? Are you okay, sweetheart?" I chose to stare at her rather than reply. She sensed the seriousness in the air. "Why do you look so tense?"

I caressed her hair and said, "Do you remember we had given our samples for a complete blood check-up this morning?"

"Of course. How can I forget that some fucker sucked my blood this morning! So what about it? Is there something to worry about?" She went on with her guesses.

I leaned over and picked up a paper lying on the nearby table.

"Sweetheart," I said with a heavy heart, "the insurance company has denied insuring you on the grounds of your illness." Saying this, I handed over that paper along with the doctor's prescription. I didn't want to extend the conversation since I was aware that prolonged talks meant more chances of the truth getting out.

"What disease?" she read from the prescription. "And three months complete bed rest! Are you kidding me? Is that why you returned home late in the evening?" she asked in a shocked state.

"Nothing serious dear. Your liver has been infected and you need three months of complete bed rest. According to the doctor, it is just a normal swelling."

"My probation is due on Monday. My manager will not approve a long leave of three months even on medical grounds. Why did you not wait for me? Why did you visit the doctor all by yourself?"

"I was already there to consult the doctor about my medicine. Just when I was about the leave from there, I got a call from the lab regarding your report and I could not stop myself from asking the doctor about your report too. Don't worry, darling! It's now time for you to resign from your job and take rest while pursuing whatever you have always wanted to do. Also, the doctor has asked you not to exert yourself."

"Oh! Is that why I have been feeling like puking all the time since the past few days?" she reasoned. She had again answered her own question, so I stayed quiet and she carried on. "By the way, is your report normal?"

"Yes, nothing significant has been identified in my report. Just a urinary infection. Oh, and the doctor has suggested I avoid sex and use protection while doing it; there are chances of you getting infected too."

She seemed really sad with my scary explanation. In an attempt to lighten her mood, I said, "It is great that all of it was diagnosed in time. But we need to bear in mind that the situation might worsen if not treated well or cared for properly. The doctors will be conducting a series of tests after three days. Until then, no outside food, no liquor, no office, and a lot of rest." I pinched her cheek and asked, "Okay?"

"This is really weird! What the fuck is happening?" she almost screamed. "My liver is infected, my job is at stake, and how on earth are we going to manage the money for our survival and all the treatment? And..." she sighed.

"And what?"

"We can't even make out! Does this have anything to do with your Goa trip?" she blurted out in frustration.

"I will handle everything, honey. Just have faith in me." For the first time in my life, I tried to convince someone with utmost confidence.

"Now what in hell does that mean?" she replied in despair.

I said puckishly. "I can use a condom."

●

Next day was Sunday. I wanted to have a word with Papa. I stepped out of the house and went straight to our society garden, a small fenced area called a 'park' by some people. Well, if people called it a park, I might as well call my flat a mansion. I sat at a corner of the park, closed my eyes and did something that only a helpless son could do. Cry! I could neither help my family, nor could I save my wife. I sobbed for the next few minutes. I called up Papa and after the usual formal talk, he asked, "How is Astha?"

"She is fine. When will Mom be home?" I lied.

"She should be here next month. What is the matter son? You sound worried."

"Papa," I said with tears in my eyes. "I want to buy a car."

"How much, my son?" Being a struggling teacher, buying a car was out of my financial capabilities. I had justified my tears well, a son's inability to purchase a car and asking for money from his father at the age of thirty-two!

"Why are you sounding so low, Vijay? It is absolutely okay for a son to ask for money from his father."

"Papa, at this age, ideally a son should gift such things to his parents, but…" I sighed, amidst sobs. "I really am an abnormal person." I had a lump in my throat.

"Vijay, please don't think like that. In today's times, a car is not a luxury, it is a necessity. Delhi roads are not safe for bikers anymore. Just tell me the amount that I should transfer."

"At least two-and-a-half lakhs."

"You'll have it in your account by tomorrow."

"Papa, you never check how I spend the money I take from you," I said partly relieved and partly surprised.

"Son, at this age, most of the fathers imagine that their sons must be having an affair or burning money on alcohol or in discotheques. I happen to be out of that lot because I don't have any such concerns. I trust my son and believe that you'd never ask for money for trivial reasons. Yes, you are indeed an abnormal son," he said, sounding emotional.

"I love you Papa."

"I love you too, my son. And one more thing, never keep any secret from your father."

"How do you know that I am keeping something from you?" I was surprised yet again.

"I am your father, Vijay. I won't force you to reveal anything until you think that it is the right thing to do. Always remember, crying with someone is way better than crying alone."

"Papa, I understand your point, but do you have that much money on you?" I asked with hesitance because my father never discussed financial matters with me.

"You know what the best part about retirement is?"

"What?"

"The provident fund!"

10

I was about to go home when I got a call. A call which gave me a purpose in life.

"Hello," I said.

"Hi Vijay, this is Sargam. How is Astha?"

"Hi Sargam, she is good."

"Vijay, is she around?"

"No, please feel free to talk."

"Vijay, I was unable to talk much when you asked me about her wishes. But I did recall one incident when I was planning to shift to Bangalore. I had asked her a weird question – ten things to do before we die!"

"What were those?" I asked inquisitively.

"Actually, she had written something but hadn't shown it to me. I am not sure what she wrote, but am sure that it must have been something very serious and meaningful because otherwise she would have shared it with me."

"Astha doesn't maintain a journal." I was thinking where those wishes could be written. Well, maybe she did have a diary! Who knows. Our relationship was only six months old, after all.

I rushed back to our house only to realize that I couldn't hunt for the diary right away, as Astha was home. The moment I stepped in, Astha fired her question, "Why do you look so lost? Did you cry?! Now I am not going to buy that you have infected your eyes as well."

My mind was too occupied with the thought of her journal to realize that my eyes were red and filled with tears. I cupped her cheeks and said, "Stop guessing, my unstoppable wife. My eyes were itching, so I rubbed them hard."

"Are you sure?"

"Of course. Why would I cry?"

She was about to say something, but I cut her short, "I have good news."

"Oh finally! Tell me quickly. I am tired of hearing only the bad ones."

"I have been promoted from assistant professor to associate professor," I lied.

"Really?!" she said and kissed me. "Congratulations, Masterji!" I thanked god that she didn't doubt how I had received the promotion call on a Sunday.

"And there is more good news coming your way."

"One more? Wow! What is it? A bumper offer?" she said and we laughed. She hugged me and said, "I feel today is a special day."

"From now on, every day will be special."

"Oh, confidence! Okay now tell me the good news."

"We are buying a car."

"Oh my god! I love you sweetheart," she screamed as she poured kisses on me. It felt like a rain of kisses. She was cheerful. Her smiling face made me emotional. I was content to see her happy. My perspective of life had changed.

"What happened Vijay?" she said, sensing my gloominess.

"I always wanted to purchase a big car, but we might end up buying a smaller one."

"We can save some money and buy a bigger car later on then," she suggested.

"Yes, we definitely can. But as per the doctor's instructions, it is unsafe for you to travel by public transport or even on two-wheelers. So we have to make the decision right now."

"I am perfectly fine with a Nano."

"Really?"

"Yes. You know sweetheart, I always dreamt of owning a Mercedes, only to realize that every car is like a luxury car if you have the best person of your life sitting next to you." She held my chin and continued, "Vijay, I'll always choose sitting with my husband in a Nano over sitting alone in a Mercedes."

●

We booked a cream colored Tata Nano and it was scheduled to be delivered in the next two days. It was Monday, probably her last day at work. I dropped Astha at the bank. As she was about to get off, I said, "Astha, please leave this monotonous job of yours."

"Bye darling," she said, giving me a 'get lost' look. She shook her head and stepped inside the bank. I rushed back home and got on to hunting for her diary. After half an hour of searching through all her belongings, I finally caught hold of a red diary. Without wasting a second, I flipped it open.

There was a page with details of Daniel's father's account. There were a few transaction details, few mobile numbers, all the passwords to her various social networking accounts, etc. One of the pages was for one of her friends, Daniel.

Daniel, I am so sorry that I cannot marry you. I am sure that one day you'll be in a state to understand me. You must be thinking that I am a lady who is chasing....

It felt as if she had broken down before being able to complete the sentence. Or, she must have been drunk while writing it. Anyway, just below the above lines was the crucial part for which I had begun my hunt in the first place.

Seven wishes before I die -
1. *Be a good mother*
2. *Apologize to Daniel*
3. *Marry either a hero or a celebrity*
4. *Host a grand birthday party with more than two thousand guests*
5. *Have a bank balance of fifty lakhs or one crore, whichever is achievable*
6. *Get featured on the cover page of a gossip magazine*
7. *BB*

It felt like a cruel joke. I wondered whether Astha was crazy or were these actually the wishes of the girl I loved. It was a tough situation. I was talking to myself; people do talk to themselves when they are tensed.

- Who is this Daniel? And why does Astha want to apologize to him?
- How on earth was I going to fulfil her dreams? We could not even have sex. How would she ever become a mother!
- Marry a hero! Really?! I am not sure about hero, but Astha has definitely married a zero.
- She wants two thousand people to wish her on her birthday? Who is she kidding! How can a person who is unable to take care of his wife host a grand party for two thousand guests!
- Become a millionaire? Astha has definitely married the wrong guy.

- Cover page of a magazine…she is neither a model, nor a celebrity. Why would any magazine publish her picture?
- And what on earth is BB? Does she mean Blockbuster Bollywood movie on her or BlackBerry?

I weighed my options and gave up. I sat on the floor and tears gushed out of my eyes, making me feel helpless again. I tore that page from her diary. In the space between '*Seven*' and '*wishes*', I wrote '*impossible*'. Now it read: '*Seven impossible wishes before I die.*'

11

I stepped out of my house. Everything seemed the same. Everyone was in a hurry. The weather was hot and humid as usual. Roads were crowded with unwanted souls. Nothing had changed. But I felt that the world was different for me now.

I started my bike and headed towards Noida to meet my father. I had no idea how my father would be able to help me and what I would discuss with him, but in my situation, he was the best person whom I could seek advice from. Millions of negative emotions and thoughts had already begun to muddle in my brain.

Should I reveal the truth to Papa? How will he react? What will he think about Astha? What exactly should I say to him? Will he doubt Astha's character?

I argued with my own thoughts. He is an old man and revealing the truth would not provide any positive outcome. On the contrary, this could be an unwelcome stress for him. Throughout my life, I have always made him worry and have not given him any reason to smile.

Why was I thinking like that, I wondered. Maybe because the worst situations in our lives bring out some unique changes in us. I didn't realize when I had covered the entire distance from my house to my parents' and in a few minutes, I was at the doorstep of our house. Mom was on a trip to South Africa to personally interview sports personalities for the upcoming, famous FIFA world cup to be held in South Africa. My dad was a happily retired man. My mother – who was five years younger to dad – had no age bar for retirement. A journalist is a journalist all her life.

As expected, my father unlatched the door and asked, "What has happened to my son? It is a Monday."

I couldn't utter a single word and hugged him instead.

"What is the matter Vijay?" my father asked again.

"I was just missing you, Papa."

"The last time you said you were missing me was when you had failed to clear the IAS exam for the third time. I hope everything is okay. Is Astha fine?" he asked me point blank.

"Yes, everything is fine."

"Vijay," Papa said, "you should avoid such long trips. Astha would get bored alone. Anyway, how was your Goa trip anyway?" I had been so occupied in my thoughts that I had totally forgotten to get him the souvenir I had got from Goa.

"Good," I replied, in my usual monosyllable.

He moved towards the kitchen to get his lunch. I was sitting and imagining how I had spent my life in this house, jumping around in every corner. I had a sense of belonging for every part of the room. I mentally thanked god that I was not staying in this house any longer as it would have meant that I would have to die here.

I began to feel that every material thing was immaterial to me because the most relevant person of my life was in a fix.

After thirty minutes of heartless discussion about food, Goa, college and my mother, we settled on the bed. I was still thinking of a way to strike a conversation about Astha.

"What happened, Vijay?" Papa asked while caressing me, "you seem worried." I wanted to hug him right then and let my emotions loose.

"Nothing much, Papa," I said giving a fake smile. "One of my friends has been diagnosed with cancer and is in the last stage."

"Ohh," he said, sadness clearly reflecting from his voice. I summoned all the courage I had in me and tried to bring up Astha's topic in a different way.

"Papa, suppose one day you get to know that Mom is about to die in a few days, how will you react?"

My question stunned him and I could make out that he had definitely not been expecting such words from me. My father is a filmy man. Actually, he is an impractical man, but I want to refrain from saying it out loud. He changed his posture and shifted towards me.

"Son, everyone who is born has to die one day. The moment I get to know that your mother is about to leave us, and that I have limited time to talk to her, I will start by apologizing to her for each and every mistake of mine and will try to keep her as happy as possible for the rest of her life. I will try to fulfil all her wishes before she dies."

"Then why wait for death, Papa? We can do it while we are still living, right?" I said abruptly. He was silent for a few seconds.

"Exactly, that is the point. If your mother is about to die, she will never wish those things or even tell me her wishes."

"What is the need of fulfiling her wishes then?" I asked inquisitively.

"A person should try to fulfil all wishes of a dying person because those are for him. At the end of the day, he will think that instead of sitting and crying in one corner of the room, he at least tried to do something for her."

"Isn't that selfish?"

"Who says that it is wrong to be selfish?" He sighed and continued, "Listen, your friend is dying. He likes snowfall and by some means you are able to fulfil his wish. Won't that give you satisfaction?"

I nodded.

"Papa, I wanted to ask you one more thing."

"You are behaving really weirdly today!" he said. I ignored his observation.

"How did you change so drastically? All your life you were a very ambitious father, but after my marriage, I have seen a sudden change in you. All these years you had been forcing me to prepare for government jobs. I still remember the way you had reacted when I had messed up my interview. Sometimes, I even felt that you were way too strict."

"You too have changed after marriage, son."

I gave him a confused look. He understood my predicament and said, "Vijay, it's not about your marriage. It is about my retirement. While I was working, I would be frustrated with my busy duty hours. A cop's life is full of humiliation, torture and disrespect. Every time I was transferred to a new place, I cursed my destiny. Post retirement, I finally got some time for myself and it was then that I analyzed life. The best thing about retirement is inner peace," he said.

"So you have finally got your inner peace?" I asked.

"How can I, when my son has lost his. Now tell me frankly what the matter is."

"How could you guess that?"

"Because for the very first time, you are asking too many questions. And trust me, your questions are difficult to answer."

"I am not hiding anything, Papa. My best friend is in trouble." I faked a yawn and turned to the other side, pretending to sleep.

"I know you are lying." I was shocked at how sure he was.

I couldn't utter a single word and hugged him instead. It was a hug by a thirty-two-year-old man who was scared of life. I was feeling light and I wished it to last for eternity. For those few seconds, I felt like I had nothing to worry about.

"What is the matter son?" asked my father while caressing my back. That was it. I broke down.

"Is Astha fine?"

"We humans spend half our lives planning on how to spend the remaining half. But we are so helpless, Papa. There are millions of things that we aspire and wish for, but it is surprising that we cannot achieve everything. We are too minuscule in this world and are helpless against destiny and god's plans."

"There are billions of things that humans can do too!" Papa was trying to give his best shot at consoling me.

"Papa, I prepared for years to get into the IAS in the wild hope of giving you some happiness. It took me only a few attempts to realize that I am a useless son. It was Mom who pulled strings for me to get the job of a professor, that too just an adhoc one. I have never had a friend in my life! I wonder how Astha landed up in my life. She is my only friend, my bundle of joy, my wife, but..." I was shivering with anger and found it difficult to talk.

"But what Vijay? You are scaring me now."

"She is slipping away from me."

"What happened to her?"

"She is HIV positive."

I narrated the entire situation to my father and he fell silent. I could tell that he was in deep thought, figuring out a way to make me feel positive.

"Papa," I said, "the moment I got to know about her illness, I took it on myself to fulfil all her wishes. But it dawned upon me that I cannot. The wishes are beyond my capacity. However, I am going to fight for all of it to come true, whether they're achievable or not."

"Why are you giving it a shot when you know it is impossible to fulfil them?"

"I would be immensely satisfied if I am able to fulfil even one of her dreams."

"That is a selfish approach."

"Who said that being selfish is wrong?" I was shocked at my own words. "I want an answer, Papa. Why is it that every single time I am the only one punished by god? I wish for a miracle to save her. Please god!"

"Stop blabbering to god!" my father shouted at me. "And stop begging for a miracle."

I watched him, aghast. It was as if a priest was saying that there is no god.

He raised his voice, "Everyone has to die someday."

"But not at this age. A twenty-eight-year-old girl who has been married only six months and wishes to be a mother, plans to purchase a house and a car, wants to live a happy life with her family – she can't die. How can her death be justified?"

"I am not justifying anything, Vijay. You are absolutely right. Tell me, how many times have you seen me happy around your mother?"

It was a weird question, coming from my father. Nevertheless, I replied, "Very rarely."

"That is the point, my son. Even after staying under one roof for more than thirty years, we rarely talk to each other, and whenever we do, we end up squabbling. Whatever time Astha has in her kitty, give her all the happiness she has always wished for."

"How Papa, how?"

"Fulfil her wishes before she leaves us."

"Her wishes are impossible to fulfil."

"Tell me, what are her wishes?"

I was hesitant to share that piece of paper with him. However, I handed it over to him. My father was shocked. The piece of paper fell from his hands and all that he could manage to say was, "Who is Daniel?"

•

He didn't say a word. We ate our lunch in silence. For the first time, I was feeling uncomfortable in my own house.

"Papa, I should get going. It's time to pick Astha from her office," I said getting up from the chair. "She was going to be terminated today, so she might need me to be by her side."

"Please wait for a minute." Papa went to his room and came back in a few minutes.

"Vijay," he sighed, "you are well aware that I joined the police force as an inspector and retired as an inspector. I gave my best at being a police officer. Even after all the good things I did, my department suspended me for four months." He gulped a glass of water.

"What are you getting at, Papa?"

"A person who believes in god always seeks for a miracle to happen that will solve all the adversities. In that hope, he ignores applying his potential to the fullest. Finally, he ends up being a loser, and the beauty of it is that he blames all of it on god. Don't believe much on miracles and god. If a miracle has to happen, it will happen anyway. Give it your maximum."

I chose not to react. He continued, "A bird resting on a tree is never afraid of the branch breaking, because it trusts its wings. Please understand, Vijay, you need to believe in yourself. Give in your best shot, my son."

I nodded. Just as I was stepping out of the house, he returned the page containing Astha's wishes. I unfolded it and read '*Seven* <u>*impossible*</u> *wishes before I die*'.

12

From Vijay's Father

This is Sanjay, Vijay's father, and I am writing for my son. I'll be filling in my version of the story in bits and parts. And let me clarify that I am writing as a father. I agree that I am a father who killed his son's confidence. It is the law of nature that the creator is the destroyer too. I created my son's life and destroyed it. As if that wasn't enough, destiny has tried to destroy it further.

My life ended with the commencement of Vijay's life. I had had a love marriage, but my love died after marriage.

During my tenure as a police officer in Uttar Pradesh, I met a passionate and very career-oriented journalist and the first flush of love blossomed in my life. She was Vijay's mother. I liked her confidence and passion. Needless to say, an honest police officer had fallen for a journalist.

Happiness and marriage were two different sets altogether. She was a complex mix of beauty and brains. My honesty was perceived by her as an opportunity to blackmail for negotiation and earn some money. Honesty was just a theory for her which had no relevance in reality.

Whenever I arrested someone, she would poke me to lower my self-esteem and sell my inner-self, and upon her insistence, I did it several times. I was no more an honest police officer. The person I would see in the mirror had died twice.

During her third attempt at pushing me to take a bribe, I was caught red-handed and was suspended for four months. My temporary suspension had put to death the permanent happiness of our life. I resumed duty but our relation could never be resumed.

We would now fight for every trivial thing, be it about my salary or posting. I cannot remember any week which passed by without a heated argument between us.

After the first few months of our wedding, I had settled with the fact that we were two very different beings and was now certain that we were not made for each other. I believe it's always better to stay alone and happy, than with someone and sad. I had almost made up my mind to quit from our marriage and was on the verge of re-writing my life when the saviour of our lives made an entry. My wife got pregnant. Vijay meant the world to me, and was much loved by both of us. We still had reasons to fight, but also one reason to avoid those fights.

The nature of my job required me to travel to different cities. Vijay's mom joined a sports magazine as an editor and that required her to travel to different places to interview the players. This hampered Vijay's studies. The absence of both parents during his formative years resulted in the weakening of his academic foundation. He started losing grades and after a few years, low grades had become the norm. He would score just enough to be promoted to the next class.

My life was totally shattered by now. There was no promotion and enthusiasm in my job because now my name had been registered in the list of corrupt police officers. My frustration of being unable to go up the ladder clouded Vijay. I forced my dreams on him. Vijay's mother and I had a heated discussion over Vijay's career. She wanted him to opt for engineering, but my frustration led me to win. I announced to both of them that Vijay would only become an IAS officer and nothing else. Surprisingly, Vijay never expressed his wish to be something else. Initially I felt he was an over-obedient son. It was later that I realized that he didn't have a consideration in any subject. He turned out to be an introvert and very shy. He would rarely speak. He had no friends; a girlfriend was out of the question.

He would hardly fight for anything. Struggle, inspiration, passion to achieve something was all alien for him. He had failed to clear the IAS exam in all his attempts. Just once, he had cleared the prelims and main exam in UP-PCS. I still remember the day when Vijay had announced that he had cleared the second paper of UP-PCS and was preparing to appear for the interview round. I was thrilled because for the first time I could see a ray of hope. I was posted in Meerut then. I took leave to visit my son.

"Vijay, my son, you are very close to fulfiling your father's dream. I am really very proud of you," I said while giving him a welcome hug.

"Thanks Papa, but..." Before he could say anything else, I interrupted him, "Do you remember what you had said when you had failed in the third attempt of IAS? You had said that you cannot do it anymore. And see, your hardwork has paid off today!"

"But Papa, you wanted to see me as an IAS officer."

"No, I wanted to see you as a PCS officer. PCS officers join the police force." I lied to him so as not to weaken his confidence.

"Why did you force me to clear the IAS exam then?" he asked.

"Because preparation for IAS, which is tougher than PCS, would have made your journey of clearing the PCS a cakewalk

for you." I was amazed with my explanation. I don't know what I had done to my child because he said the same sentence that haunted him the most.

"Papa, the interview is still pending."

"I know Vijay. I am confident that my son will clear it with flying colours," I assured him.

"But I am really scared, Papa."

"Scared of what?"

"The interview."

"It is all about being confident."

"That is the point, Papa. Confidence is exactly what I lack."

"Vijay, look at our neighbour's son Mohan. He had failed twice in his tenth standard exams, but still managed to clear the PCS."

"He belongs to the SC category. He had the advantage of reservation."

"We have Yadav uncle's son as well."

"He is an OBC." His answers frustrated me.

"Don't compare yourself with others, just look at you."

"I am a general category candidate."

"But you are very special."

"Stop comparing my son with any Mohan or Sohan," Vijay's mother shouted and interrupted our conversation. She would always do that – interrupt while I spoke to my son.

"I am not comparing him with anyone. And he is my son too," I retaliated.

"Vijay, don't listen to what he says," said his mother.

"Can I talk to my son in solace?" I snapped at her.

"Remember Sanjay, he is the only son we have," she said before leaving the room.

I wondered how she had landed up in my life. Her presence had changed the air completely. Few minutes back we were behaving like Krishna and Arjuna. The silence now felt like we were sitting in a mortuary. This was a very common scene in our house.

"Vijay, don't listen to your mom," I said exasperated.

"Mom says not to listen to you and you say the same about her." I wasn't surprised with his words because this was not the first time that Vijay was facing this situation.

"Focus Vijay! I am not comparing you to anyone. I am cent percent sure that you can make it. When is your interview scheduled?"

"A month later."

"Now listen carefully. Join the best coaching institute to help you prepare for the interview. I will personally conduct your mock interview."

"Okay Papa, as you say."

That was the problem with my son. He always pursued others' wishes. His biggest problem was that he could not face more than two people at a time. I was myself worried about how my son would manage the civil services interview with a dozen eyes staring at him, all at the same time. I cannot say that my son is a loser because after all, he is my son and, like every father, I had the right to hope for my son.

His final interview was scheduled in Allahabad. I had reached Noida a day prior to my departure for Allahabad. I waited patiently for my wife to leave that place before I could step in.

"Vijay, let's practice with a mock interview," I said, wishing to gauge his preparation.

I aligned five dining chairs in a row, with one chair facing them. These chairs were the panelists' chairs and the opposite one was the candidate's chair.

"Vijay, just imagine that you are in the real interview board room and five panelists are interviewing you."

"Oh, five people!" exclaimed Vijay.

"Focus Vijay, look into my eyes. There could be more than five panelists. What difference does it make?"

"It scares me, Papa."

"Don't worry. You can do it. Just relax. Be comfortable. Now let's start your interview. You wait outside the room and enter when I ask you to."

"Okay," said Vijay. While opening the door, he asked, "Sir, may I come in?"

"Please, Mr Vijay, kindly come in and take a seat," I said while flipping through the pages of the telephone directory. "So, Mr Vijay, where are you from?"

"I am from India, currently residing in Noida," he gave a sharp and positive answer.

"Nice. I am impressed. Tell me something about yourself."

"I know the answer, Papa. The coaching institute already gave me the best lines to say when asked about myself."

"Vijay," I raised my voice, "Answer me. You are in a board room!"

"I am Vijay. I studied in a convent school throughout my education. I hail from a highly respectable family. My father is working as a police officer with the UP Police and my mother is a leading journalist. Love for our nation and people flows in my veins. I have been an achiever throughout my life. I have always achieved whatever I dreamt of. In my college cricket tournament, I was always appointed as an umpire because the teachers were impressed with my honesty and decision-making skills. I will put these skills to use and go to any extent to serve my nation."

I was really amazed and wondered if these lines were indeed for my son or someone else.

"Great answer, my son."

"Papa, we are in a boardroom."

"Oh, I'm so sorry. So, Mr Vijay, why do you want to join the police force?"

"Whenever I see or hear any news regarding the UP Police for all the wrong reasons and imagine people feeling unsafe, it hurts me. After all, I have seen my father sprinting from place to place just to serve the state, and even after all that, the situation is stand-still. I always wondered when this system will change. It was then that I realized that dreaming will not change anything, but becoming a part of the system definitely will. As a human being, it would be the best feeling to punish criminals and help people feel safe."

I began clapping as it was difficult for me to believe that he was the same Vijay, my son, who was afraid to even open his mouth in front of other people. "You indeed joined the best coaching class," I pampered him.

"Thank you, Papa. These are all standard questions for which I am thoroughly prepared. But..."

"No ifs and buts after this, Vijay. I am now assured that you'll fulfil your father's dream."

●

On the interview day, I was more tensed than him because he was chasing my stupid dream. The thought that he would freeze in front of unknown people worried me. I was praying since morning and as soon as Vijay called me up after his interview, I jumped off my chair hoping to listen to one of the happiest news of my life.

"How was the interview?" I jumped straight to the point.

"Good."

"Really? How long did it last?"

"Around five minutes."

"What? How many panelists were there?"

"Ten."

"Oh my god!" I was silent for a few seconds as I was getting negative vibes. "Vijay, what did they ask you?"

"They asked only three questions."

"Three! I am sure you must have answered them confidently."

"I tried my best."

"What was the first question?"

"Tell me something about yourself."

"Great! You'd have said the same lines as yesterday, right?"

"Yes, I tried."

"What about the second question?"

"Tell me something more about yourself."

"What?" I was shocked. "And the third?"

"Anything else that you'd like to tell us about yourself?"

●

I vividly remember the day Vijay visited me. It is the best feeling to have your son hug you, but it turns to the worst feeling when he has tears in his eyes. He was disappointed, disheartened and dejected. I could only blame myself. Yes, I was the one responsible for the state Vijay was in.

If a child has poor self-esteem, it is because you advise them more than you encourage them. If a child lacks confidence, it means you have never allowed him to take any decisions. Vijay was in this state because of bad parenting.

When he failed in all his attempts to clear the IAS and PCS, he had come to me and cried his heart out. He had cursed god. But in the heart of hearts, I was fully aware that I was to be cursed. I was the one who had expected the unexpected from him.

His mother beat the odds by recommending him for the post of an assistant professor and got Vijay a job. We then decided to marry him off. Even after a wild hunt for a year-and-a-half, we failed in all our attempts. But every cloud has a silver lining. I often wonder how a girl like Astha gave her consent for a boy like Vijay. They were an imperfect match then and they are an imperfect match now. Astha is bold and Vijay is shy. Astha is confident, cheerful, ambitious and modern. But she loves him earnestly. It is always a blessing for parents to see their child being loved, adored and cared for by their spouses.

Happiness in Vijay's life doesn't stay for long. And this gave rise to another Vijay – he fought for his wife. And now that she has been diagnosed with HIV, he has somehow reaped the courage to chase her weird, almost impossible wishes. Only a person in love can attempt to be so foolish.

But for a father, it hardly matters whether his son wins or loses. I was content with the fact that he was finally fighting for something. I promised myself to walk with him every step.

I moved to that section of the almirah in the bedroom where the divine deity resided in idols, whose existence was still doubtful to me. "Oh god!" I said, "Please help him accomplish all her wishes. My son's behaviour can be considered as madness but at least provide him with courage and confidence. Please god, help my son. Help me."

13

Astha was already home when I got back.

"How did you get home early? I had asked you not to commute by public..." Before I could finish my sentence, Astha hugged me tight and started crying like a baby. It was a repetition of what I had done with Papa. Only this time, I had to be the confident one. I had to be her rock; I couldn't afford to be weak.

"Hey," I said consoling her, "What happened?"

She chose to be silent, which was abnormal for Astha.

"How did you get home early, sweetheart?" I asked again. She was still buried in my arms.

I loosened my grip around her, cupped her cheeks, looked into her brownish eyes, and asked gently, "What happened, Astha?" I was a bad actor, but she was too sad to notice my hopelessness.

"Vijay, I lost my job."

"Oh!" I said sympathetically, but quickly added, "Well, don't you see it? Finally some good news! It has happened for the good. It is destiny's way of telling you that it is high time you chase your dreams."

"I fail to understand what is going on around me," she sobbed.

I chose to ignore her remark and picked up my college magazine which was lying around. I held it up for her to see and said, "You can be a writer."

"Writers are the least paid, Vijay."

"Astha, I want you to be a writer because you wanted to be one at some point in time. Remember, it is not about the

73

money. When you get a job, millions of others do the same thing as you do for a living. But you have the sole custody of your life," I philosophized.

"Vijay, is that really you? You are the not the same person." I shrugged and frowned while she continued, "But what about our expenses?"

"You don't have to worry. I have been promoted, remember?"

"Mr Vijay Sharma! You are behaving as if you have become a millionaire overnight. What increment have they offered?" she remarked sarcastically.

"Forget about all that. What did your idiot boss say?"

"You know what, for the first time in my duration at Axis Bank, I saw my boss regretful of making a decision. When he apprised me of my probation result, I could easily sense the pain in his voice and the sad look on his face only confirmed my doubts."

"Firing an employee is always painful."

"Yeah, I guess so," she said and sighed.

"Now listen carefully," I said gearing up, "don't try to travel by public transport again. I am very serious about it."

"I didn't travel by public transport, Vijay. A colleague dropped me home."

"Oh! Who?"

"My boss, Mukul Mathur."

●

Next day, I called up Sargam to enquire about Daniel.

"He was a common friend of ours," Sargam lied. I knew, because the description from Astha's diary was non-compliant with Sargam's answer. It was difficult for me to get Sargam to spill the beans.

"Listen Sargam," I said with utmost patience, "I hope you are not treating me as your best friend's husband. I am your friend too and you can tell me the truth because I know that Daniel cannot be just a friend."

"Actually," she said hesitantly, "Daniel is her ex-boyfriend."

I was not surprised, because for a girl like Astha, her not having a boyfriend would have come as a surprise to me. I asked further, "Where is he nowadays?"

"He is currently working with Barclays Bank in Gurgaon as an investment banker."

I wasn't sure of what I was about to ask, but I still tried to face it. "What could possibly be the reason that Astha would need to apologize to him?"

"Because she decided to marry you without even informing him. Daniel was studying at California State University then. He had requested Astha to wait for him until he got back. But Astha had made her decision. Daniel is a Roman Catholic and his family wasn't ready to accept a Hindu daughter-in-law."

I felt nothing. No desperation. No sadness. I had no idea how to react. I stood calmly and mustered the courage to shoot my next question at Sargam, the most difficult one. "Are they still in contact?"

"I am not sure, Vijay. Daniel returned to India the same day you married Astha."

"Do you have his contact details by any chance?"

"Yes, I do. But I'll share them with you only under one condition."

"I am ready for anything."

"What exactly is wrong with Astha?"

"I'll tell you, but only if you promise to keep it to yourself."

"I hope you are not treating me like Astha's best friend. I am your friend too."

14

Astha's seven wishes had started haunting me. It had been six months since I had known her, but it suddenly felt like I didn't know her at all. How could a modern and ambitious girl like her wish to be a mother? There ought to be a reason.

After a sumptuous dinner, we were relaxing in front of the television. A news channel flashed that Sushmita Sen, a famous actor, was planning to adopt another girl child. She was not even married. Being a single mother must have been so difficult, I thought. Her courage intrigued me to ask a dangerous question which most men dread to even think about.

"Astha," I said hesitantly, "I think it is time for us to extend our family."

"Oh my god, Vijay. That's great! Mr Vijay is finally ready to be a father!" The excitement in her voice was in sync with the spark in her eyes.

"Yes, I am thinking of adopting a child."

"Adoption!" she said. "Why adopt when we can conceive one?"

"Astha, there are many orphans in our country. So instead of making an addition to the already growing population, we should adopt a child."

I am not a saint, but the reason I presented for adopting a child had definitely categorized me as a stupid man, at least to my wife. As a reflex action to my words, she frowned, mumbled something and finally she said, "No, I will not adopt a child."

"Why?" I countered. "What is the big deal in adopting a child?"

"Nothing, I just don't want to."

"Are you hiding something from me?" I was fully aware that the chatter box that Astha was, she would surely tell me what was on her mind.

"I was a step-daughter for my father's second wife, and when she had a baby girl, everyone shifted their focus from me to her. Whenever my mother went out to shop for something, she would buy stuff only for my step-sister. Every year, her birthday was celebrated like a carnival. No one would even wish me on mine. Only my father would occasionally gift me a few dresses. I protested, only to realize later that I had always been an unwanted child – an unwanted illegitimate child," Astha said with tears in her eyes.

I hugged her tight and said, "As I had told you when we first met, it is not the child who is illegitimate, but the parents." How difficult it must have been for her to put up a smiling face. Who could have guessed from her happy-go-lucky nature what she had been through and will be going through!

"I know that," she said composing herself. "I am not at all responsible for what my parents did. But Vijay, throughout my life, I have remained confined to myself. I never had anyone to hug. You can never imagine the plight of a motherless child. I always wished to have shown my idiotic mom..." She went silent.

"What Astha?" I said holding up her chin.

"That one day I will be the world's best mother."

Her sentence gave me a mini heart-attack and for the first time, I decided to lie to her on her face. "Of course, you will be one."

"What if we give birth to a child after adopting one? We might not be able to avoid differentiating between the two." Her fears were coming forth now.

"I am sure we will love both of them equally. Suppose we don't have our own baby, then adoption is the most feasible option." I cursed myself the moment these words slipped out of my mouth.

"That's right. If you use this fucking condom every time we make out, then we'll end up only with an adoption," she said in despair. I smiled.

"Why are you laughing?" And again, she had considered my smile to be a laugh.

"Nothing, I am sure of one thing." Making someone happy with a lie is always better than hurting them with the truth. "You'll be the best mom ever."

15

Although I had no doubt that Astha's love for me was pure and unadulterated, I was a human being who could go weak at times. I had Daniel's number and wanted to speak to him, but was wondering what I would say. I wanted to meet him too, but somehow had a bad feeling about it. So, to be on the safer side, I took an appointment with Daniel for Sunday. I introduced myself as Sargam's friend who wanted to speak about something essential. He was insistent that we meet in his office, but after a few persistent requests, he agreed to meet at his house.

I noticed a strange psychological change in myself. I had suddenly become more outgoing. Whatever I did, I did it without any fear or inhibitions, maybe because I didn't have anything to lose.

I unfolded the page on which her seven wishes were written. I smirked and said to myself, "My dear weird wife, why could you not have more common wishes? You must probably have been drunk or insane while writing this."

I wanted to try everything that could give her happiness. I failed to understand why I wasn't giving up as I had always done. I made up my mind to work upon the next impossible task.

I called up Sudha aunty, the editor and chief of *Hype & Dust* magazine, and ended up at her office. Being a journalist's son, it was cakewalk for me to dig out Sudha aunty's contact details. She was a close friend of my mother's but had snatched my mother's story once and was no longer in her good books. Surprisingly, she had turned up during my wedding and it had appeared as if they had resolved their differences.

Hype & Dust was the leading gossip magazine in the Delhi NCR area. They were amongst the top five when it came to distribution. Their office was small yet presentable. A few seats were placed in the waiting area. I settled down in one of the chairs and flipped the pages of a magazine placed on a nearby table to kill my time while I waited to see her.

After a few minutes, I stepped up to the receptionist's desk and asked, "Can I have a look at the previous issues of the magazine?"

"Sir, we have a small store for visitors. Feel free to walk in." She pointed towards the coffee machine adjacent to which was a room labelled 'Magazine Repository'. I found multiple copies of each month's issue of *Hype & Dust*. I had a glimpse of their cover pages – that was my only target.

"Astha, one day your photo will be on the cover page of this magazine!" I promised her in my heart.

Most of the cover pages featured common men, projecting their rare quality – a debut author along with his book, a few struggling models, a young successful entrepreneur, some leading brands, creative artists, a famous philanthropist, a restaurant owner, leading advocates and so on.

Some issues of the magazine had pictures of sexy ladies teaching you five methods to make wine at home. Yet another story featured a housewife teaching one to make rotis that remain soft for three days. A couple's picture clicked in complete darkness featured an article on the importance of sex in married life. My eyes were locked to the next article – 'AIDS cannot kill love'.

Each time I picked up an issue, my confidence only heightened. I was now sure that only Sudha aunty could help me fulfil at least one of Astha's wishes.

After an hour of waiting, I was called inside Sudha aunty's cabin. The famous Mona Lisa painting hung on one of the walls, of course a copy. The second wall was adorned with antique showpieces of a black lady, a few photos with famous celebrities like Dr A.P.J. Abdul Kalam, Shahrukh Khan and Salman Khan. The third wall was covered with awards and recognition received in appreciation by *Hype & Dust*. It was a room with massive hoo-ha – a showoff of prosperity and money being her slaves.

"Welcome Vijay. Long time no see."

"Hi aunty!"

"How are you doing? How is Sushma?"

"Mom is fine, aunty. She is still in South Africa for the football World Cup coverage."

"Call me Sudha, please. Do I look old enough for you to call me aunty?"

I guessed that she was infected with the rare psychological disorder of not being able to accept the truth of aging. I smiled.

"How is Astha? Well, I must say, you have a gorgeous wife," she said playfully. I considered it wise to get straight to the point before she said anything related to my sex life.

"Sudhaji, I need a favour."

"Please feel free to ask for anything. I'd love to help you."

"One of my close female friends wishes to be featured on the cover page of your magazine."

"So you want *Hype & Dust* to feature a story about her?"

"Exactly," I said, nodding my head.

"Tell me more about this friend of yours. What does she do? Is she a model or a director?"

"She is a common lady."

"Okay, let me guess. An ordinary lady who wants to publicize herself to boost her business or modelling career?"

I was amazed by her guess.

"Kind of, she is a budding writer," I lied.

"Five lakhs," she said, as if she was carrying a menu card.

"You charge for it?" I said aghast. She nodded and I continued, "So all those stories about businessmen and common man becoming uncommon were paid stories?"

"Don't think of it as paid. It is PR. After all, it helps boosting their business."

She triggered another storm in my mind.

"How many books has she written?" asked Sudha aunty.

"She is working on her first book," I lied again.

"The charge for debutantes is eight lakhs."

"What!" Had Astha been there, I am sure she would have said 'fuck you' on Sudha aunty's face.

I had a similar urge while she continued, "Featuring a debutante is always risky. Had anyone other than you approached me, I wouldn't even have considered their offer. But I don't want to disappoint my friend's son."

Her generosity was too much to digest. Firstly, she made me wait for more than an hour and later offered a discount of millions!

"So Sudha," I removed the ji from her name because she had lost it right in front of me. "All these writers whose photos have been featured on the cover page paid you to get there?"

"Yes. Not just us, almost every other magazine has this arrangement. A minimum of ten lakh rupees is charged for a cover photo and four-page story. You must be aware that we have a circulation of close to one million copies in the city."

"My friend is not that rich. To tell you the truth, I had come here with a request. She has been diagnosed with HIV and always wished to be featured on the cover page of a magazine."

"Oh, that's great!" Her rising excitement at someone's plight bewildered me.

"Excuse me?"

"We can surely publish her story."

"Really?" I was confused.

"Yes, we would feature a cover page story on her along with the tagline – hate the sin, not the sinner."

"What is the relevance of that?"

"We'll write a story wherein we will project that your friend was sleeping around with some men, or male prostitutes for that matter, and had unprotected sex because of which she got infected. Now her last wish of seeing herself on the cover page of a magazine will be fulfiled. *Hype & Dust* will help her. I'll publish my photo with her."

"But that is not true!" I said irritated with her remarks. "There are other mediums that can infect one with HIV."

"Such as?"

"Such as an infected syringe, infected blood transfusion, breast feeding, drug addiction from a common syringe, shaving with the same blade, any small cut from an infected knife or blade..." I could go on but she cut me short.

"But all these reasons cannot cook a story. It won't sell."

"But this is the matter of someone's life."

"But for me, it is business."

"Thank you." I could not waste any more of my precious time. But I guess she didn't get the implication of my thank you.

"Listen Vijay," she said, "this story can do wonders. I can get my magazine sponsored by a condom manufacturer. My proposal is totally free. Think over it again." Her enthusiastically popping eyes were reflecting greed in its purest form.

"Thank you for your time. Let me tell you something, Ms Sudha. You magazine's name is perfect."

"Oh, thanks. I created it."

I sighed. "It is only hype and dust!"

16

We were sitting outside Dr Raza's cabin, waiting for our turn. Yes, I had got Astha with me this time. After all, she was the patient.

"Vijay, Dr Raza is a very senior doctor. What's his consultancy fee?" Astha enquired with concern. Only a lower middle class person can think about money while in the hospital, rather than the disease.

"Nine hundred."

"That is pretty expensive!" she exclaimed and waited for my nod and I had to oblige as a duty of a husband. "Why are we wasting our precious money here? I am totally fine," she added.

"Let the doctor say the same thing and I will be convinced. Also, I am planning to appoint a full time care-taker for you at home."

It was really difficult to convince Astha for any kind of expenditure. It is not that she was a very unwell patient, but she couldn't be blamed; the symptoms of this disease were rarely visible.

"I only have a common cold and—" her sentence was cut short as her name was called out.

Dr Raza didn't seem to be in a hurry. We were not the last patient either. Before he said anything, I probed him, "Sir, this is Vijay. I hope you remember me. And this is my wife," I said pointing at Astha. "As per your instruction after seeing her report, I have apprised her that her liver has been infected." Astha gave me a weird look.

"Of course. How can I forget you? I do remember everything," replied Dr Raza. I heaved a sigh of relief.

"Doctor, I am totally fine. My husband is unnecessarily worrying about me."

"Astha, your husband is not worrying unnecessarily. It is good that there are no complications with your infection currently. You have been diagnosed well in time. But it will only get worse if you don't take care of yourself. Now tell me, do you feel drowsy, itchy, have a common cold, pain in the part of the abdomen near the liver?"

"Yes, doctor. Since the last few weeks I have been feeling very drowsy, and have been experiencing mild pain in the lower abdomen. But I guessed this was because of the medicine."

He threw a glance at me and said, "I guess so."

I passed him a smile and added, "She has cold since the past twenty-five days."

She nodded in confirmation.

"What about the last couple of days?" asked Dr Raza.

"I have a metallic taste in my mouth. I often feel like puking."

"This indicates that the medicines I prescribed have been effective." Saying this, Dr Raza mumbled the names of some medicines. Doctors and astrologers always throw difficult words at people. "Astha," he continued, "I require you to get a full body test conducted so that I can gauge the seriousness of the infection."

He started writing something, which was Hebrew to us. I guessed it included a complete blood profile test, involving thyroid, metolic, pregnancy, H++, haemoglobin, ultrasound, TLC, CD3and CD4 cell count, urine culture, CT Scan, X-Ray, kidney tests, among others.

86 ♥ *Ajay K Pandey*

"If money is a constraint, then CT Scan and ultrasound can be skipped at the moment, but everything else is mandatory. It is Friday today, please get all these tests done and visit me with the reports on Monday."

"Doctor, Vijay is too concerned. Please tell him that this is not required at all."

"We will discuss that after we have the reports in hand," Dr Raza said.

"Okay, thanks."

"Vijay, you'll have to monitor her diet. No processed food. No wheat flour, rice, pasta, potatoes, tomatoes, beans, maze, legumes, eggplant, or dairy products. Instead, give her lots of protein, veggies, fruits, nuts and seeds. You have to treat her like a child."

"Why a child?" Astha asked.

"We decide everything for a child, from the food he eats to his sleeping timings. Everything needs to be monitored closely. The same goes for you. A careless attitude can change your fate. Until then, enjoy your time."

She watched the doctor aghast.

"Vijay, how is your UTI infection? Kindly avoid sex for a few months as it could affect her liver." Dr Raza lied and smiled, "You can use a condom though."

These words from the doctor's mouth were enough to scare the hell out of Astha.

●

The same night, I was sitting in our bedroom reading our college magazine *The Spark*. It was ironical that no spark was left in me.

I didn't have the money to fulfil her wishes. I didn't have money to celebrate her birthday. I didn't even know whether she would be alive till then or not. The expense of the treatment was the only prime thing on my mind for now. However, I was adamant on meeting Daniel.

"What are you doing Vijay?" Astha interrupted my chain of thoughts.

"What happened?"

"You have been holding you college magazine for the last fifteen minutes but I am sure you are not reading it."

"Oh, is it? Well, I was thinking." I faked a smile.

"No wonder! These days you think a lot."

"You know Astha, in the past, I had appeared many times for the IAS exams. Most of the time I would not even check the result. But I would still appear the next time because Papa would push me to do so. He had his own motives to do that."

Astha realized the pain in my voice. She came close to me and kissed me.

"I know that sweetheart. But why are you thinking about it all of a sudden?"

"Every time I failed to clear my exam, I would be disappointed. I would cry. Each time Mom would walk up to me and apologize on Papa's behalf. She would say that Papa loved me a lot and wished to accomplish his own dream via his son's accomplishments. Mom had realized that it was impossible for me to clear the IAS exam."

"Does your Mom know what an apology is?"

"Stop it, Astha! She sure did. I feel that she was more sensitive towards my feelings than Papa."

"Really!" she said sarcastically.

"You'll realize it someday," I said with conviction and faith.

"I don't think so," Astha said pretty insensitively. "But why on earth are you thinking about all this?"

"Sweetheart, I am wondering whether it is ethically or morally correct for a wife to seek an apology on behalf of her husband."

She thought about it for a second and said, "It is not about husband and wife. It is about the love they share."

I realized that it was dangerous to ask for advice from an extrovert, but I took a chance. "Please explain."

"Anyone who loves the other person can seek an apology on his or her behalf. For example, you love me and so you can seek an apology on my behalf." She had managed to hit the bull right in the eye. That was exactly what I had wanted to hear. I gave her my stereotypical smile.

"Why are you laughing now?" There it was! The same question again. But by now I had excelled the art of ignoring this question by asking a counter question.

"What if a person doesn't forgive the other person?"

"Winners always forgive whereas losers always retaliate. The person who apologizes in turn passes on all of his burden on the other person's head. The one who understands this always forgives. Whereas the ones who seek further revenge only burn themselves daily by having to bear all the burden. And according to that logic, my husband is a winner."

"Oh okay." I showed her a thumbs up as a sign of my appreciation and asked, "How am I a winner?"

"Because you have forgiven your father."

17

I reached the address Daniel had given me. I found two cars in the parking lot, a Maruti which his father would have used and a Diesel i20 which I assumed was my wife's ex-boyfriend's.

I rang the doorbell. A tall, smart, handsome young man – who bore a mature look on his face, wearing frameless spectacles, shorts and a t-shirt with 'I Love USA' embossed on it – welcomed me. All the confidence which I could never have screamed from every part of him. I wondered whether he was the same person whom I had come to meet. My doubt vanished when I heard a heavy American accent.

"Hi, I am Daniel."

"Hi Daniel, I am Vijay." I was feeling awkward. The usual question popped up in my head, yet again – how did Astha end up marrying me?

"Hi Vijay, please come inside and have a seat."

He was clearly a very sophisticated and well-mannered person.

"Feel at home," he said. "What would you like to have? Tea, coffee, or juice?"

"Whatever is convenient for you," I said.

He went inside. His house wasn't big, but at the same time it seemed to be owned by a wealthy person. The sofa was new, and the living room was tastefully done. There were pictures of Jesus and a golden cross indicating Daniel's strong faith. Daniel was back at his seat in a minute's time.

"Yes Vijay, you told me you wanted to discuss something personal. But before that, may I ask how Sargam is? It has been a long time since I last spoke to her."

"She is doing well," I said. I was wondering how to initiate a conversation about Astha.

"Are you married, Daniel?" I had no idea why I asked this question.

"Not yet," he replied. Meanwhile, two glasses of juice along with cookies were served by the maid. I decided to open up fast, else the investment banker would lose interest in me. I began narrating a story which I had made up.

"Daniel, I made a terrible mistake. Last week I met with an accident. In order to save a kid on the road, I drove over a pedestrian in front of a church and the person got hurt. No one noticed since it was very late at night. However, I was not completely responsible for the accident. So I didn't fear anyone and called up an ambulance to attend to the patient. I also visited the hospital in which he was admitted. One of his legs had broken and may take about six months to heel. Although I am not sure whether he will be as fit as before."

He was as sharp-minded as I had expected him to be and said exactly what I was hoping for. "How can I help you in this?"

"Sargam had apprised me that your family has a strong belief in the Bible. The guy who was hurt is a Christian." For the first time, I looked right into his eyes and said, "I want to apologize for the accident. Could you, by any chance, find me a lesson from the Bible so that I can seek an apology from that person with a legitimate reason?"

My dull face was in complete sync with my narration. "Well, in that case, it is my father who you should speak to," he said while sipping the juice. "Let me call him here."

"Oh no. I'll be awkward talking to him. I am sure being a religious person, you would definitely be able to help me."

"I have less knowledge of what you are asking of me and am not a religious person at all. However, I know that the basis of Christianity is forgiveness. The people who had killed Jesus were forgiven by Jesus. Even when we go to church, people confess to the priest. I suggest that you visit a church and confess your guilt. Also, it would be better if you could compensate the hurt person with some money or anything you deem fit. That should be enough."

"But what if he retaliates?"

"Vijay, it is the losers who retaliate. Winners always forgive. I am sure he will forgive you." I was surprised how he had shared the same philosophy as Astha.

"But," Daniel said looking at me doubtfully, "I can sense that you are hiding something from me."

"Yes Daniel, you are right. In our Hindu religion, husband and wife are considered to be partial owners of each other. Just like assets belong to both, so do responsibilities."

"You seem mysterious. What is the point Vijay?"

I took a deep breath and said, "Do you remember Astha?"

"I know that opportunist very well."

I was puzzled. "Opportunist?"

"Yes, she was my girlfriend until a few months back. Then she got married to a professor. But why on earth did you mention her name?"

"Please allow me to complete what I have to say. Daniel, Astha approved of marrying a professor under family pressure. Given that you belong to a different religion, it was difficult for her to convince her parents."

"I cannot believe that," Daniel seethed in anger. "Astha would never listen to her family. Anyway, if that is the case, she could have waited for me to return to India or spoken to me."

"For all her mistakes, she has been feeling sorry."

"I doubt it. She leapt on the opportunity of marrying a rich guy. She is an emotionless girl who has never loved anyone." Daniel was seething with anger.

"How do you know that her husband is a rich man?"

"He has to be. I know Astha very well. I have heard that her father-in-law was a senior police officer and her mother-in-law is a journalist."

"In that case, you don't know them."

"But why are you talking about her?"

"Do you think I am a rich man?"

"Who are you?" he asked raising his voice.

I sighed. "I am Astha's husband."

He looked at me dumbstruck. His jaw fell. His trance broke after a few seconds of silence. "How dare she send you here?" he said, his voice still raised. "You have come here to mock at me, isn't it?"

"No Daniel. I am here to tell you that my wife is sorry for her mistake of not fighting for you both. In short, she is sorry for running away from the situation."

"And why should I believe you?"

"Because that is the only reason for which I am here."

"Had she been really apologetic, she would have been standing here in front of me."

I went silent as I did not want to reveal about her illness.

"Why is she not here?" he almost shouted while I still remained silent. "Vijay," he continued, "the day she dumped me was the day I vowed to meet her and prove that she had committed a huge mistake. I have fifteen POs reporting to me at the bank. I have an apartment in Gurgaon. Very soon I'll be marrying an IAS officer's daughter. Astha is a fiasco to have dumped me for you!"

I chose to remain silent instead of picking up an argument with him because he had all the right to say all this.

"Daniel, she really is apologetic for what happened."

"Then why is she not here?" he repeated.

"Because she is unwell."

"Mr Professor, let me admit that you are amazing at cooking up stories. But I am not your student. Please leave now."

I stood up, but I wanted to make one final point.

"Daniel," I said, "we cannot change the past. Currently, there is no way in which you can soothe your anger. Jesus had forgiven even those who led him to death. I hope you try to understand her and forgive her."

"I am not interested in talking to you or her, the bloody loser!"

He was in a rage. I was standing at his doorstep ready to bear his frustration. "Get lost, please!" he shouted loudly.

As I stepped out of his house, I said, "Don't call her a loser, Daniel!"

He pushed me mildly. I moved out of the house and he shut the door behind me.

I said, "A loser always retaliates."

●

It rains once in a blue moon in Delhi. Today, it was raining. I love the weather when it rains. And today, I too contributed to the rains. The best thing about crying in the rains is that no one can notice your tears. I felt defeated in idiotically chasing nothing.

Why am I doing all this? I am so dumb. I should be dead like I have been for all these years.

I cursed myself. The pain I felt was not because of Daniel's words, but because of my continuous failure.

I stood under a tree while tears continued to flow from my eyes. I looked up at the sky and murmured, "What did I do wrong? Why is my wife going through all this?"

I pulled out that paper of her wishes from my pocket and threw it away. *This is all rubbish. Henceforth I won't try to fulfil any of it.* In short, I had given up. And it wasn't the first time.

My cell phone rang. Though I was not in a mood to answer any calls, I answered when it rang again.

"Hi Vijay, this is Dr Raza."

I was not in a state to hear anything from the doctor. But I still had to, for the sake of my wife. I answered in a half dead state, "Hi Sir."

"Vijay, please ask Astha to stop all medication with immediate effect. All her test reports have been delivered to me. Pay me a visit tomorrow and please come alone."

"Is there anything serious?"

"Nothing to worry, Vijay. I am just unsure whether this is a good news or not. Your wife is pregnant."

I hung up without any formal greetings. I went numb. I was in a state of shock. It was one of the weirdest moments of my life. A doctor had called up to inform me that I was soon to be a father and he didn't even congratulate me. I didn't know how to react. Should I be happy or sad? I was completely blank. Everything around me was moving while I was standing still. Just one question loomed over me – what if the baby gets infected with HIV?

I looked at the crumpled piece of paper that I had thrown. I picked it up, unfolded it and read it to myself.

I smiled while tears were still trickling down my cheeks. The smile was for an obvious reason. One of the wishes of my wife was about to be fulfiled. My score was 1/7.

18

"Doctor, I don't want this baby."

I had two reasons for taking this decision. Soon after being born, the child would be motherless for the rest of its life. Or, it could be infected with HIV too.

"I can understand." I knew that it was not an everyday situation for him so chose to explain it to him.

"I just don't want my baby to come into this world with a terminal disease and in turn suffer his or her entire life."

"Vijay, I can understand your concern, but Astha's pregnancy report says that she has been pregnant for more than three months. We cannot do an abortion now. If we do, we'll only end up risking Astha's life because Astha's CD4 count is less than 400 and it will only reduce with time."

"Doctor, what are the chances of the baby being infected from the mother?"

"Honestly, there is a fifty percent chance."

I went numb again. The doctor continued, "A few cases have been observed wherein patients have delivered a healthy child." His words clearly indicated that he hadn't handled such a case before.

"Doctor, I don't want to have this baby. Should I consult a gynaecologist? I do not have the strength to see another one of my own die in front of me."

"Why are you only thinking negatively, Vijay? There is also a fifty percent chance that the baby is totally healthy."

"What about the remaining fifty percent, doctor? It is okay for a doctor to look at the positive, but impossible for a would-be-father to even dream."

"I agree with you." He said with modesty. "I suggest that you consult a gynaecologist too."

"Do you know anyone who has handled a similar case before, and who will be ready to help me?"

"Yes, I know one. By the way, I have already discussed Astha's reports with her. If you want, you can also consult Dr Rachna."

"So in her previous case, was the delivery successful?" I had to be sure.

"No, that was not a successful birth. The child had died... but she is a good doctor."

I began thinking.

"Dr Rachna will keep the secret, you don't worry." Dr. Raza's words broke me free of my trance.

"Which one?"

"She will not tell Astha about the disease." I had forgotten any such thing.

"How are you so sure that she would help me?" I asked.

He heaved a deep sigh and said, "Because she is my wife."

•

Why did Astha keep the news of her pregnancy hidden from me? Was she not aware? But how can a lady be unaware of her own pregnancy? Is this baby even mine?

It seemed like a movie with an invisible villain. I wished for it to be a three-hour movie where everything would be back to normal after stepping out of the theatre. However, my biggest worry was the climax of this movie. One problem had not even ended, and the second one had cropped up.

Whenever I am confused, there is one door I knock on. I headed towards Noida.

"Papa, I have some news for you."

"What is it? Good or bad?" Whenever someone asks this question, be sure that they are ready for the worse.

"I am not sure. I haven't classified it as yet."

"Okay. Tell me. I am up for anything."

"Papa, Astha is pregnant."

"Oh!" I was unsure whether his exclamation was with happiness or shock.

"Why do you say that Astha is pregnant? It is not just her who is going to have the baby, you are going to be a father too!"

I followed this with a detailed description of my tete-a-tete with Dr Raza.

"Are you happy, Papa?" I said while ignoring his remark. I was not mature enough to digest the fact that he hadn't congratulated me yet.

"No, I am not happy. And I do have a doubt," he said.

He looked at me with love and said, "Don't get me wrong, but are you sure this baby is yours? Given that she is an HIV patient and you have been travelling much in the past. What if it turns out that you don't know her completely?"

The same doubt had culminated in my mind a few minutes back, but I couldn't accept anyone doubting my darling's character. I sighed and said, "Papa, Astha has been pregnant for about three months and it has been six months since we got married."

He looked at me aghast. I said with tears in my eyes, "Even if by any chance what you are saying is true, it is a child growing in my wife's womb. That is enough for me to call it my own."

Papa hugged me as silence prevailed in the room. Both of us needed this hug. For the first time I felt like I wasn't alone after all. I sensed that he was on the verge of breaking down too. We freed ourselves from the hug. I saw respect in his eyes after a really long time.

"Vijay, it is high time that you inform Astha about her condition. She is in need of complete care now. She will anyway get to know the truth with the frequent visits to the doctor and while being treated. In fact, the more you delay informing her, it will only be dangerous for her...and now for the baby too."

"Papa, I will be okay if it is revealed to her naturally. I want to avoid confronting her myself."

"What nonsense is this, Vijay?"

"I don't have the courage to tell her. I have already faced the worst and am sure I can face this too."

My father was silent. He thought for a few seconds before saying, "You have gone through the worst."

●

I purchased half a kilo of rasgullas from a nearby sweet shop and stood outside my house. The door was only a metre away from me, but I found it difficult to take those steps. I didn't want to tell her the good news with tears in my eyes. I pulled out my shades and wore them for quite a different reason.

With a heavy heart, I rang the doorbell.

"Why are you wearing shades?" she asked concerned as I walked into the house.

"Something has gone into my eye and it is hurting. Anyway, I have some good news for you," I said beaming.

"Really? Good news?" She didn't seem as excited and cheerful as she used to be on the prospect of hearing some good news. She didn't even notice the packet of sweets.

"Here, take this," I said while handing over the packet of rasgullas to her. "I got your favourite sweet." She took the packet from me and headed straight to the kitchen.

Should I tell her that she has been diagnosed with HIV? How will she react if I tell her the good news, which won't be good anymore once she is aware of her condition? I couldn't decide. After a few minutes, Astha stepped out of the kitchen and filled my mouth with one full rasgulla.

"Hey, let me tell you the good news first."

"Remove these shades first," she removed the goggles from my eyes.

"Astha, you are pregnant."

"That's not fair! How did you get to know?"

What a reaction! I had expected her to be excited, but this was the opposite.

"Your reports were due today. Dr Raza called me up and informed me of this great news!"

"My dear husband, I have known this for the last thirty days. I learnt of it when you were in Goa. I had planned to surprise you and was on the lookout for the right occasion." Saying this, she hugged me emotionally. She had tears in her eyes. I was about to cry too, but couldn't afford to be weak in her presence. However, I couldn't decode the reason for her tears.

"I love you, my dear soon-to-be-mom." I hugged her tighter and closer.

"I always wanted to be a good mother. You cannot imagine how satiated I am." She sobbed and continued to bury herself in my arms while tears trickled down my face.

I concluded I will not reval the truth.

19

My college vacation was now nearly over. My mom had returned from South Africa. She got the news of Astha's pregnancy, but she didn't care to call her.

Astha had to visit the hospital every alternate day. The CD4 and CD3 tests were compulsory for her, twice a week. Meanwhile, the progress was good. Her condition was stable and she did not show any signs of worry. She often vomited, felt weak and I helped her as much as I could with the cooking, cleaning, laundry and grocery shopping. Dr Rachna helped us a lot, and no one was discriminating. I was glad that everyone was treating her like a normal human being. I had to hide all the medical prescriptions and reports, especially those that carried the name of the disease. She didn't ask for much, she was living peacefully at home. The kind of girl that she was, it was difficult to make her stay at home all the time. However, she made no request to join any part-time job, though her main concern was the family expenses.

Even after two weeks of regular treatment, there weren't any improvements in her CD4 count and it was pretty low. It worried the doctor and he recommended a strict diet along with vaccination, monitoring her blood pressure, and taking her blood sample on every alternate day. College was about to open in a week and all these things were too complicated for Astha to handle alone. I discussed the matter with Dr Raza and he suggested appointing a full-time nurse for her.

Astha was concerned about the expenses more than her health. She was taken aback by the doctor's recommendation as we could not afford a full-time nurse. But my spirits were up. I was ready for the next challenge. This time, it was the nurse. I didn't want to run from one hospital to another and get disheartened. I asked Dr Raza about the some agency that could provide nurses at home.

Next day, I was sitting inside the Caring Nurses Consultancy, the tagline of which said 'We care for you'.

It was just a small office, comprising a small cabin and an open waiting area. A man in his forties was sitting inside. A few nurses in uniform were waiting at the reception. They might as well be looking for a job, I thought. The receptionist was busy talking on the phone and it was only after a few minutes that I got her attention.

"Sir, how may I help you?"

"Do you deal with providing qualified nurses at home?"

"Yes, we are pioneers in that service. We are the largest nursing consultancy here."

She gave me a form to fill, which asked for a few necessary details, like the patient's name, gender, age, disease, consulting doctor, nature of the disease, contagious or not and if it was a terminal disease. It also included questions like does the patient have any mental illness? Will any other person be available at home? Can the patient handle his or her urine and stool?

There was a small note at the bottom – 'PS: All this information will be kept confidential.'

"Ma'am, before filling this form, I want to have a word with a senior person here."

"Sir, wait for a few minutes, our counsellor will address you."

"Who is the counsellor?"

"He is Dr James Francis." She pointed towards the man who was sitting behind the transparent wall inside the cabin.

I was wondering if I should inform them about the disease. *How will they react?* I was called in after ten minutes.

Mr James wore a white coat like a doctor. I failed to understand why he was dressed like a doctor. It was not a clinic and there were no patients.

"Hi, please be seated," he formally asked pointing at the chairs placed before him.

"Hi, I am Vijay."

"I am James. Doctor James Francis," he answered as though he was James Bond.

"Actually, I have come here for a part-time nurse for my wife."

"We are the largest in personal nursing in Delhi/ NCR, and around a thousand nurses are already on the job through our agency. All our nurses are well qualified and have a nursing degree certified by the Indian Nursing Council (INC). Twenty percent have a doctoral degree in nursing," he said in one sentence like he had practiced it a million times.

"That's really great." I faked a smile.

"We are very economical. You have come to the best place," he continued boasting like he was the owner of the biggest outsourcing firm in the country.

"Well, my patient is suffering from a terminal disease."

He stopped blabbering, took a deep breath and said, "Please do not worry, our nurse will help the patient with stool and urinating, bathing to vaccination, and IV fluids as well. They treat patients like their own relatives."

"No, I don't require such things. A nurse just needs to help her with her injections and daily routine activities. She has to monitor her blood pressure. There is nothing more that is required. She can walk to the washroom and perform the daily activities on her own."

"Great. I can arrange a couple of nurses you can interact with for the job right now. What is the name of the disease?"

"It's HIV."

"AIDS!" he said shocked. He thought for few seconds. It was difficult to believe he was the same person who was unstoppable a few minutes back. I sensed that he was not going to help me.

"Mr Vijay, I forgot to tell you that we don't manage patients with contagious diseases."

"HIV is not a contagious disease; it doesn't spread through touching, hugging or even by kissing."

"Vijay, I am sorry I cannot help you. We cannot put our nurses in danger."

"But there is no danger. I am myself staying with her, sleeping with her and I am not HIV positive."

"It's not our concern who you or your wife sleep with," he said arrogantly.

"Hold your tongue! You cannot talk to me like this," I shouted. It was the first time I had shouted out so loud.

●

After an hour, I was standing in front of the next nurse consultancy center. Its board read 'Care@Home'.

This place was situated in the district centre of Jasola. Apollo Indraprastha Hospital was just a kilometre away. I went inside. It was bigger and more crowded than the previous one.

"I am looking for a qualified home nurse." I briefed the lady sitting at the reception.

"Sir, please be seated, we will call you."

I was expecting some form would be given to me that needed to be filled, but this care centre seemed a bit different. One silver board said – *We are not here for the money. We are a non-profit organization.* There was a poster of Jesus next to it. I read the next one:

Dear god, it is my misfortune that my income is related to people's pain and disease. But give me strength to fulfil my duty towards mankind.

I was highly impressed.

"Sir, you can go now," said the receptionist.

I entered the inner cabin. The name plate said, Thomas Pereira. Another Christian in a row after James. This industry was full of them and I failed to understand why.

"Hi, Pereira sir. I am Vijay."

"Welcome Vijay ji, please take a seat. Before you explain your requirement, let me tell you certain things; we are not here for money."

"That is really great."

"Our intention is solely to serve humanity. We are a non-profit organization and have qualified and certified nurses only." He sang the same song which I had heard a while ago. Somewhere deep, I felt it was going to be the same story all over again.

"Sir, I know yours is a very efficient organization. Please, listen to my requirement first," I butt in, not wanting to waste any time.

"Oh, I am sorry. Feel free, we will keep all the information confidential," he said.

I explained my requirements and informed him about the criticality of the disease, without revealing the name. And added at the end that an economical one would be better.

"Don't worry about the charges. We will charge you the minimum. I told you we are not here for the money. Now, what was the name of the disease?"

"Sir, my wife is suffering from HIV."

"HIV ... you means AIDS?"

"There is a difference between HIV and AIDS, but yes you can say that."

He went silent for a minute. It was not an unexpected reaction to me.

"Vijay, a few months back, one requirement came with the same concern. He interviewed a few nurses but no nurse agreed to work for him."

"Sir, please understand. I need your help. Please try at your end."

"There is only one way. We will need to hide the illness from them."

"How is this possible? The nurses will ask for the doctor's prescription."

"Vijay, everything is possible if you have the money. Don't worry about the doctor's prescription. I will manage it for you. You only need to give me a little extra amount for getting a fake doctor's prescription."

"How much?"

"Ten thousand."

"What? Ten thousand rupees only for writing some disease on a doctor's pad!"

"I am not charging for the doctor's prescription; I am charging to hide the disease and get you a nurse."

"This is too expensive."

"It's your wish, Vijay. What I know is that if you tell any nurse that your patient is HIV positive, no one will touch her, leave aside taking care."

I didn't like him from the very beginning, but after getting kicked out from the last place, I was sure he was, at least, making sense and could get me a nurse. I was thinking about my next move when he smiled mysteriously and said, "Mr Vijay, my intention is to help you. We are not here for money."

"Okay, but what will they charge? I want them only for six hours."

"It depends on the nurse you choose. The more qualified and experienced will charge more. But it varies from twenty thousand to fifty thousand. Charges also depend upon the nature of the job. Suppose if there is any bleeding or external injury involved, the charges are higher. If washing and cleaning of the patient are included, you will be charged extra. Over and above, all hand gloves, cotton sheets, and syringes would have to be purchased by you."

I was not comfortable with anything he said. He understood my position, got up from his seat and patted on my shoulder.

"Vijay, don't worry. If your patient can manage her washing and cleaning, then it should not be more than twenty thousand. Okay?"

"Okay. Can we conduct the interviews today? Malviya Nagar is a bit too far from Jasola."

"Wait, let me check." He went outside and came back after ten minutes with a few papers stacked in his hand.

"Vijay, you are lucky, as two nurses are available right now. Here are their CVs."

I was looking at the papers and trying to read which one was more suitable for her, but I was interrupted by him.

"Let's talk to them first." I nodded and he called the first one in.

Radha Gupta looked like a girl in her late teens. She was very thin and I could not believe that she could take care of anyone else. It seemed she herself needed a nurse.

Both of us stood in front of Thomas. It looked like I was being interviewed by Thomas.

"Tell me something about yourself," Thomas asked. The question gave me chills.

I countered and asked another question, because I felt that question was not required. "Radha, how many years of experience do you have?" I asked another question.

"No experience. This will be my first."

"Why should I hire you?" Thomas fired the second question. I was impressed by Thomas as I could not think of any question.

"I know all the necessary vaccinations and nursing responsibilities. During my studies, I've worked in a hospital." Radha was replying in one liners. I guessed it to be her first interview as well.

"Vijay, do you want to ask anything?" Thomas poked me.

"I think she would be fine for the job."

"Great. So do you have any questions, Radha?"

"I have a few reservations," Radha said. "I would not like to work at a place where the patient is having a contagious disease like tuberculosis, viral fever, flu, an open wound or AIDS," Radha said.

"But AIDS is not contagious." I protested.

"I know, but I don't want to work for an AIDS patient," Radha responded.

"Okay, Radha! This patient is suffering from jaundice," Thomas said.

"It's perfectly fine then."

"You may wait outside," Thomas ordered.

She went outside but I was in no mood to appoint her.

"I don't want this nurse."

"You will not find any nurse for an HIV patient," Thomas said to convince me.

"I have a question. How can a nurse take care of the patient when they are not aware of the disease? Suppose a jaundice patient is suggested to have grape juice; what if that grape juice is harmful to my wife? What if it puts her life at risk?"

"Then, what should I do?" asked Thomas.

"Call the next nurse, I will talk to her."

"Next nurse is a bit expensive."

"It doesn't matter."

After a few minutes, Rosy Gomes entered. Rosy was a middle-aged, confident looking lady.

"So Rosy, how many years of experience do you have in nursing?"

"More than ten."

"Just to check your knowledge, what is the difference between HIV and AIDS," I asked.

"HIV is the carrier and AIDS is a fatal disease. An HIV patient can live a normal life if taken care of properly, but an AIDS patient cannot live long."

"Good," I was impressed. Then I asked the question that was to be decisive. "Is HIV contagious?"

"No, it is transmitted only if there is blood contact and unsafe sexual contact."

Her answers relaxed me a bit.

"Sister Rosy, I don't want to hide anything, and as you know AIDS is not even a contagious disease, my wife is an HIV patient and she is pregnant. Could you please extend your care to her?" I literally crossed my fingers this time.

"No," she said without even a second's delay. She was clear about everything she didn't want.

"Why, what happened? There is no risk," I almost cried out.

"Sir, I had taken care of an HIV patient in the past, and when everybody came to know that she was an HIV patient, they started treating me like an untouchable. They acted as if I had the infection. Since then, I have decided I would not be part of any such treatments."

"Thanks, you may go now," I said irritated.

After she went, Thomas was a bit worried and suggested, "Vijay, hire the first one. She is still not aware of the disease."

"But hiding the disease will be risky for the patient as well as the nurse."

"You can pay more. It's worth the risk."

I felt irritated.

"How can the money dissolve the risk, Thomas?"

"Money is everything; people are ready to take risks because of money."

"Suppose I give you one crore, can you remove all risks from my wife's life?"

"Vijay, you are getting me all wrong; my intention is to help you, and we are not here for money."

"No, Thomas. I think you are here only for money."

20

Next day, I went to meet Dr Raza with another problem. He was not just a doctor now; he was my counsellor and guide too.

"Vijay, you can work as a nurse," he suggested.

"How I can work as a nurse?" The thought had never crossed my mind.

"It's very simple. What are we expecting from the nurse? To inject her twice, monitor her blood pressure, and take her blood sample on every alternate day along with proper care and support. The care and love which a family member can give cannot be compared with any paid nurse."

"Is it that simple?"

"Yes, that's all. Go to the pathology department. There will be a lab superintendent Mr Ravikant Gautam. Inform him that I have referred you; he will guide you about how to inject and monitor BP. You'll learn it in a day or two at max."

"Thank you, doctor."

"My pleasure. But she requires constant monitoring. How are you going to manage your job with it?

It was rare for me to exhibit confidence, but I knew I had no choice.

•

We both understood that the baby would require all possible care and her pregnancy would not be an easy one. Astha had to take care of herself for the health of the baby. She had been advised to meet Dr Rachna every five days. Few tests were compulsory on a regular basis. Her CD4 was to be monitored on every alternate day. Astha accepted all her instructions, and her condition stabilised. But a pregnant lady with AIDS is a rare and dangerous combination. I explained to Astha that nurses were slightly expensive, so I was her new nurse. She smiled. I wanted her to smile for the rest of her life.

Astha never asked any questions. She did not look for another job. The girl who loved to drink and eat non-vegetarian food changed completely. She was okay with bland food day after day, without making faces. Earlier, she used to laugh; now she smiled. My wife had begun to change.

She had become weak and often felt drowsy. It was the sixth month of her pregnancy. My new assignment as a nurse took most of my time. I had less time to focus on my job and needed to talk to the principal.

"Is the principal there? I want to meet him for a few minutes," I asked the principal's secretary.

"Please wait, let me check." A secretary always knows where the boss is; she was perhaps checking whether he wanted to meet me or not. After a while, I entered the principal's cabin.

"Welcome Mr Vijay. It's a pleasure to see you," the principal taunted.

"Sorry sir, I have been really caught up. My wife is unwell. But I had informed the admin staff."

"What happened to your wife?" he said coldly, more as a formality than out of concern.

"Sir, she is pregnant," was all I could reveal to him.

"Oh, that's a very big problem," he taunted again.

"Sir, she is pregnant and her liver has an infection that can be fatal. If she is not well cared for, I may lose..."

"Oh, my best wishes are with you. So is she okay now? he asked, without much interest again.

"No sir, she is not. That's what I wanted to talk to you about. I need a favour." He nodded and I told him, "Sir, she requires care and monitoring all the time at home as she has become extremely weak. There is no one to help, so I will be able to give only limited time in college."

He made a face, and asked point blank, "What would be your maximum availability?" he asked point blank.

"I will be available only for three hours a day and need one day off in fifteen days. I have to take her to the hospital for a complete check-up every fifteen days."

He thought for few seconds. "Vijay, in that case, we can give you only half the salary, as you are coming for half the day only."

"Thanks sir." I smiled, I was not expecting much, and money was the last thing on my mind. Only Astha and my baby were the priorities for me.

"Vijay, you rarely teach anything. I don't know how I am going to utilize this time. Listen, on the 8th of November, we have our annual college function. I want you to take charge of the preparations. This time, it will be telecast live, and if all goes well, maybe we'll have the HRD minister as our chief guest."

"Sir, I will try my best."

The 8th of November was Astha's birthday. I wanted to say no to the responsibility, but remained silent.

●

I was busy taking care of my wife. I avoided my Saturday's trip home. Papa and Mom called me daily at different times. It was rare for them to sit together and talk. Papa came home a couple of times to see Astha. My inability to go out and my Mom's ego to not enter my home had kept us away for a long time. I was sure if Mom came to know of Astha's infection, she'd find another reason to hate her.

Astha and I chat every night about our past and our future. It felt weird talking about the future now. But we were happy in our imaginary world. Sometimes reality sucks.

In the second week of September, Papa came over to our house and wished me a happy birthday. Mom came to Malviya Nagar in the evening to wish me. We are a crazy family; both of them were to come from the same place, but they came separately.

Mom hates Astha, Astha hates mom, and I love both of them. It's common in Indian families, I guess. Mom called me to Pizza Hut, half a kilometre away from the house. The moment I saw her, I wanted to hug her and cry. I restrained myself, for she would guess something was wrong.

"Hi Mom," I touched her feet. "Missed you a lot." It was really difficult to hold back my tears. Her presence was making me weak.

"How are you, Vijay?"

I didn't say anything. I hugged her like a little kid. I wished I had never grown up. I wanted to shrink in her arms and die there. Finally, the dam broke and tears flowed down my eyes. My mother noticed that. It was not the first time I had cried in front of her.

"Vijay, are you okay?"

"I am perfectly fine, Mom. Just missed you a lot. Why have you called me here? You could have come home."

"So finally you have learned to lie. Is Astha okay?"

"Are you concerned about her?"

"No, I am concerned about my grandchild. Is she still dominating you? Or have you started using your brain?"

"Mom, stop criticizing her..."

"Oh, still the same henpecked husband! Thank god, I decided to meet you outside, otherwise you would have not even offered me tea."

"Mom, please. It is not only Astha's home, it is mine too."

"Why has Astha left her job?"

"She is expecting, you know that."

"If everything is fine, then why are you not going to college regularly? Your principal called me."

"Mom, the truth is that Astha is unwell as her pregnancy is not normal. A lot of care is required. She is on complete bed rest. Every small thing – from buying vegetables to medicines – has to be taken care of by me. Plus the visits to the doctor." I sighed and decided to change the topic. "Forget that, what have you brought for me from South Africa."

"This is your birthday gift," she said giving me a packet. I opened it and found a pair of wrist watches.

"A pair of wrist watches! One for Astha?" I asked playfully.

She glared at me and we dug into the pizza. She shared her experience in interacting with famous celebrities and funny things about them. I told her some funny things about Astha, and Mom told me about Papa. I was smiling after three months. Like there was no worry in my life. That moment was a mirage in my desert.

"Vijay, you are my only love in this world. I assume everything is fine with the baby. If there is anything or any help required, please let me know. I want both of you to be happy."

"Who both? The baby and me?" I asked deliberately.

"I have not forgiven her for taking away my only child from me." She heaved a deep sigh, and her eyes were wet. But I knew she was a tough lady. She said emotionally, "It is better that you are staying away but living happily, rather than staying with me and fighting every day."

I didn't know where I got the courage from, but I said, "One day, you will forgive her."

21

"Vijay, let's eat out tonight," she proposed to enjoy the evening together and celebrate my birthday.

"Astha, the doctor has prohibited you from going out, remember?" I said.

"Vijay, I spend all my time watching television, listening to music, reading the newspaper and talking on the phone. Do you want to bore me to death? The hospital is the only place where I go, and the doctor is the only person I see when I go out." I could see that she was annoyed.

"Okay, let's go out, but you will not eat anything from the roadside, okay?"

"That's fine. I can do that. I need to get some fresh air. I feel as if I am caged and it's very suffocating. I don't want you to celebrate your birthday inside the house."

We decided to go to Pind Balluchi in Hauz Khas Village, famous for its Punjabi cuisine. The ambience was amazing. We found a corner table and I ordered two glasses of buttermilk. We settled on a vegetable biryani.

"Where is my gift?" I teased her.

"I am sorry, Vijay. You didn't allow me to go out, so I could not get anything for you," she played along.

"The best birthday gift is to have someone in your life who knows you so well. When I was young, I used to ask my parents to bring birthday presents for me whenever they visited me. What about you? How did you celebrate your birthday?"

"Birthday!" She gave a sarcastic smile and raised her eyebrows. "My step sister's birthday was a huge party, but mine was never celebrated. I wished to have a birthday like that. I wanted it to be huge... Grand. I was very silly."

"Go on! I want to know more," I asked as she tasted the biryani.

"Throughout my life I wanted a huge birthday party, where thousands of people would wish me, sing birthday songs for me, raise a toast for me, dance with me and I am the centre of attraction, but..."

"But?"

"But...now I feel that the best way to celebrate your birthday is with your close ones. It is better to have a few close heartfelt wishes than a thousand unknown."

"Why the change?"

"Maybe because I have found a loving person like you," she said emotionally and I also felt a lump in my throat.

"Now, I have a question for you." I tried to change the subject.

"If you have to apologize to someone, then who would be that person and if you have to forgive anyone, then who would that be?" I didn't want to put her in the tough spot, but I needed the answer.

"Our mothers!" she said as if she was ready for this question since ages. "I want to forgive my mother, and I want to apologize to yours."

It was a double shock. First, I was not expecting my mother's name, second I was expecting Daniel's name.

"I will forgive my mother since I am happy; the past is the past and I don't want to carry any grudges. Someday, we will forget the pain, the reason we cried and who caused us that pain. After all, what matters is not the first, but the last chapter of our life, which shows how well we ran in the race. So smile, laugh, forgive, believe and love all over again."

"Aren't you a philosopher!" This was a different woman. I didn't know what had changed her – the baby or the disease. "But why do you want to apologize to my mother?" I asked in disbelief.

"You know, I have never apologized to anyone. I never do that as a habit, even if I realize that the fault is totally mine. But when I conceived, I realized I cannot live even a single day without my baby," she said with tears in her eyes. "There's nothing in the world that is more important than our child."

"Please, it's my birthday!" I wiped her tears and took her hands in mine.

"I want to apologize to your mother because I took her son away."

●

"It's all because of that biryani; I told you not to go outside. It's very difficult for you to take control of your temptations. Please get ready, we are going to the hospital right away," I was angry and scared at the same time. Astha had complained about a pain in her lower abdomen.

I quickly reached the car and waited for her to come out. I started the engine but could not stop thinking about the situation. I was petrified because it was a fatal disease and any new change could be really bad. I remained silent throughout the journey to the hospital.

I stood in front of the doctor. Astha was lying on the bed. Dr Rachna suggested an ultrasound. When the nurse took Astha for the ultrasound, I started talking to Dr Rachna.

"Doctor, how is she now? Is she okay?" I asked worryingly.

"The situation is under control. She's more than seven months pregnant, so it could have been worse. She might need to stay here until the delivery." I let out a sigh of relief.

After a few seconds, the doctor added, "I have some good news."

"Good news?" I said in disbelief.

"Dr Raza had discussed Astha's case at an AIDS seminar in Delhi with a team of doctors, and they are interested in helping her out. They want to study her and try their treatment."

"They want to study her case? Are you going to do experiments on her?"

"It isn't a bad thing; these doctors are from the United States and have experience in similar cases. They have some research scheduled in India and I discussed Astha's case. They have agreed to help her out."

"Can they cure HIV?"

"No Vijay, these doctors will study her condition and then help her in delivering a healthy baby," the doctor said. There was nothing good in it for Astha.

"I see. Doctor, I am more concerned about her health. She's my priority."

She nodded in empathy. "Please wait outside. I will call you when I get the reports."

I was thinking about what the doctor had said. I was waiting outside the cabin. Astha was in the room, resting. Dr Raza and Dr Rachna called me inside his cabin to discuss the situation. The reports were ready. Being a couple themselves, they could understand what I was going through.

"Listen, Vijay!" said Dr Rachna. "She has developed an infection in her stomach, and we need to admit her. I will recommend you to keep her here till the birth of your child. Will that be okay with you?" I could see the concern in her eyes.

"Okay. But why?"

"Because any small change can harm her. We will run some tests and share the reports with the specialists through Skype. To make sure that we do everything as instructed, I would recommend you to hospitalize her for the time being. I will also need an authorization letter signed by you."

"I don't have any problem signing any authorization letter, but I think it will be an expensive treatment."

"Yes, but apart from the expenses, there will be another problem."

"What is that?" By now I was familiar with the word 'problem'.

"I want you to be strong. If she delivers the baby through c-section, then there's a possibility that she might not be able to recover from it."

"What is that supposed to mean?"

"Listen Vijay, her immune system is deteriorating every day. If the need arises to go for a cesarean, it will be very difficult for her to recover. Her CD4/CD8 ratio and WBC count is low, and if it doesn't improve, then it will not be possible for us to stop the bleeding. There is a chance that she won't be able to make it through the operation."

Her words shattered me. I became numb. I knew that one day she would leave me forever, but what I didn't know was that the day would come so soon.

"We will try our best to help you out. If everything goes well, we might be able to deliver a healthy baby."

"Okay, doctor. But you have recommended hospitalization for the next two months. It will be very expensive."

"I won't charge any consultancy fee; that's the best I can do for you right now."

"Thanks. Do you have any idea how much it will cost me?"

They thought for a while and said, "I am not sure about that. Please go to the accounts department and check with them. A rough estimate is around twenty to thirty lakhs."

"Thirty lakhs? God!" I was dumbstruck.

"If you want, you can share the room with another patient. It will save you some money. Although I would not recommend that as people will discriminate against her, since she is an HIV patient."

He continued, "I can understand that expenses are a problem, and I can refer her to a government hospital if you want me to."

"Is it possible to treat her in a government hospital?"

"That you have to decide, Vijay."

'I will not let her go. I will fight,' I said internally

I signed the letter of authorization. That said if any mishap happens to her, then the hospital, doctor and staff won't be accountable.

I told Astha that she needed to stay there until her delivery. She was not worried at all. Though I didn't tell her anything about the expenses, she could easily guess that it would cost us a bomb. I asked her not to worry and instructed the nurse to take proper care of her. I told her I'd beback in the next few hours. It was weird, but she didn't ask me where I was going.

22

While pursuing my graduation in Allahabad, I had been to Swaroop Rani Government Hospital once. A friend had met with an accident and we ended up hospitalizing him there in emergency. His injured legs were operated on the next day. Initially, the doctor had said only a few stitches would be needed, but finally he ended up losing his left leg. It was my last encounter with any government hospital.

Though this had happened ten years ago, and this was not Allahabad, this was Delhi. Delhi has many established government hospitals; some of them even meet international standards. The affordability and my patient's need to be hospitalized for more than a month had compelled me to go to a government hospital. Considering the fact that a lot of patients come to a government hospital, I was quite sure to encounter an experienced hand in my second faceoff. I decided to evaluate whether they were good enough to be considered as an option for her treatment.

I surfed endlessly for the best government hospital in Delhi without any further delay, and I found one. Before visiting them directly, I thought of giving them a call and trying to obtain some basic knowledge about the doctors and their consultancy timings. I went to the contact section of the hospital's website, and to my surprise, there was a separate section – 'AIDS enquiry'. Three landline numbers were provided. I thanked the Indian government for being sensitive enough to HIV/AIDS patients.

I dialled the first number. No one responded. I dialled again for the second time and then the third in vain. It irritated me.

"What is the use of sharing a number when no one is there to pick up the call?" I yelled in frustration. Maybe I should wait for some time and try again, I told myself.

I redialled after some time; finally, in the fourth attempt, the phone was answered by a lady.

"AIIMS," the voice said. She did not show enough courtesy to introduce herself.

"I have been calling since the last one hour."

"Who are you? What is your query?" she ignored my remark. She seemed to be in a hurry, as if I had called her in the middle of her nature call.

"I am looking for information on treatment of AIDS patients."

"Come to the hospital's OPD, make a *parchee* (receipt) of the patient and you will get the information about the doctor."

That was all that the insensitive lady said before she hung up on me.

She had disconnected the call. One hour ago, I was thanking the Indian government, and now I was cursing them. It was just the trailer; the full movie was yet to be seen. It was definitely going to be a nightmare.

I still have to try, I convinced myself.

●

I reached the hospital's OPD counter where queue numbers were allotted to the patients. There was a vast sea of people. There were ten counters and each had about a hundred people in queue. A security person was busy arranging the line and monitoring people. He carried a bamboo stick and was swinging it like he was the owner of the hospital.

"Sir, is this line for OPD?" I asked him.

"Go back to the line," he almost barked like a dog.

He was actually behaving like a mad dog. I was afraid if I stood there for another few minutes, then I would have to be hospitalized here for rabies!

I was not even sure if I would manage to get a token number before that happens.

I was walking to and fro, observing the countless number of people. There were lots of scared faces. Every single face in that line was there for a problem. But one of the faces was chewing paan like a buffalo. I was afraid; my first encounter had been with a dog and now this buffalo was staring at me. His eyes had a strange hope that I could not understand. How could a person see hope in a hopeless person like me, I wondered.

He neared me. "Do you want an OPD number?"

"No, I came here to watch a movie."

"Don't be irritated brother. You are in a ghanta hospital." He drawled his mouth filled with paan.

"Ghanta hospital?" I repeated, seeking clarification on what he actually wanted to say. He spat the red coloured liquid from his mouth and said, "Government hospital. If you want, I can help you with an OPD number now."

"How?"

"Let's have tea outside."

"Please explain right here if you want to. I am not in a mood to have tea," I was skeptical about his behaviour.

"Okay, then come to the corner with me," he said, pointing towards the staff parking area; we went and stood in between two cars. I had a bad feeling about him, but I did not have the courage to stand in a queue, without even a guarantee of getting a token number.

"How can you help me?"

"One thousand bucks for the OPD number."

"One thousand! Government charges only five rupees."

"In five rupees, you have to be here from 3.00 a.m. and wait till nine or ten o'clock to get a token."

"What!" I exclaimed. "All these people have been standing here for so long?" It was unbelievable.

"Yes, do you think they are here for movies?" he said with a grin. "You should feel lucky that you have the money," he smiled mischievously. "One thousand and you can avoid standing in the damn queue."

"How do you know that I have the money?"

"I have been doing the same thing for ten years; you came by car and parked the vehicle in VIP parking." This was the first time someone was giving me respect, but for all the wrong reasons. "Sir, if you want the token, tell me immediately. Don't waste my time."

"Okay, but how will I be assured that..." Without even listening to me, he reached into his pocket, took out his cell phone and called someone. He discussed something which a normal person can never understand.

"What is your name and age?" he asked, looking at me from head to toe.

"I am Vijay and age thirty-two."

"Doctor or department name."

"Looking for a gynecologist."

"Gynecologist," he repeated to the person hearing on the other side of the call.

"It's done. Give me the money. I will come with the OPD slip."

"No, first show me the slip."

"Just give me five hundred then. I have to pay his share immediately. The rest can be paid later."

I made the payment, my fingers crossed. I was amazed at how money can reduce our struggle. The situation takes a complete U-turn if you have money. But why didn't he ask the name of the patient? Is he coming with a blank slip? What is the name contact info of the person? Was he making a fool of me?

The buffalo with red lips appeared after fifteen minutes, his high-held head stiff with confidence. He neared me and showed me a piece of paper. I was cross-checking the details in the paper when he snatched it.

"First pay me the remaining five hundred rupees."

I made the payment and while looking at the paper, I read out.

"Patient name – Vijay and age 32."

"At least, thank me," he was beaming with confidence like he had just sworn in as the CM of Delhi.

"But the patient's name is Astha. I am not the patient."

"You said Vijay."

"You didn't ask for the patient's name, you asked mine."

"Boss, I cannot help you now."

"You have to return my money."

"No, I can't. You can do one thing, edit Vijay to <u>Vijaya</u> and it will serve the purpose."

"What about the gender. How can a male patient be referred to a gynecologist? Now, don't suggest cutting off my weapon too," I said furiously.

He uncapped his pen, struck off 'M' and wrote 'F'. "No one is going to check sir."

"Why?"

He smiled with his red lips and said, "It's a government hospital."

23

I was reading the OPD slip:

Patient's name: Vijaya, age: thirty-one and sex F, Gynecologist. It had a small line –

Chhota Parivar Sukhi Parivar. – a small Family is a happy family

It was making me insane. How to handle this upcoming thing?

I argued internally. Vijay, you've come here to evaluate the feasibility to carry out the treatment for Astha. So, you should go ahead and check the facilities.

It was crazy to go to the gynecologist without the patient. Only a crazy husband in love can do that.

I asked a lady dressed in a white coat, assuming her to be a doctor.

"Who is the best gynecologist here?"

"Dr Shefali Kalia, room number thirty-two."

"Thanks."

"But she is not available."

"Oh, is she on leave?"

"No, she only takes cases of ministers, MLAs, judges or VIPs. She will not entertain you."

What! I couldn't believe what I had just heard. These were people who could afford any big private hospital easily. I changed my question, "Who is the best doctor available?"

"Visit room number fifty-three."

After a few minutes, I was sitting outside the room. I gave my papers to the assistant while I waited outside.

I looked around. A few pregnant ladies were being escorted by their relatives. Few of them were there with their mothers, some with their husbands. There were posters with advertisements about the necessary precautions to be taken during pregnancy.

One advertisement highlighted the importance of a thalassemia test, another advertisement talked of the importance of iron intake. It showed a red colored medicine. There were many such posters all around.

There were a few moaning loudly with pain. Some were even lying on the floor in the waiting lobby, unable to stay seated due to their ailment. They looked like poor villagers. If anyone wanted to see the real poor and helpless India, this hospital was the best place to catch a glimpse of them. I found a lady sitting on the floor. I watched her as she opened her tiffin box, with four kids hovering over it. One person sitting beside me was constantly threatening and instructing them to behave nicely.

"How are you related to these kids?" I asked the person while waiting for my turn.

"These are my children," he said proudly.

"How many kids do you have?"

"Four."

I was confused whether I should be happy or sad.

"How is this doctor? You must have been here before."

"This doctor is really good. Each of my children was born here," he said in affirmation.

"Why are you here now?"

"Actually, my wife is pregnant."

"Again?" There was complete silence for few seconds and the guy was blushing like a pumpkin. With huge effort, I said, "Congratulations."

My number finally came, after two hours. I settled in front of the doctor. One lady, somewhere in her thirties, was also sitting in front of me. She was a patient. I waited for the other patient to leave so that I could speak to the doctor alone, but that was not to be as many patients were hovering around the doctor's seat. The assistant was instructing each one of them with their queries. Most of them had a few common questions: where to take the medicine from, which room to go to for tests, which room for reports, and when do they need to come again.

"Where is Vijaya?" asked the doctor while checking the sheet.

"Ma'am she is not in a position to come." I had brought Astha's reports to show her.

"What is the problem?" she asked still looking at the second patient. "Tell me, I am listening." I realized she was actually asking me. She was looking at the other patient and talking to me. It was impossible for me to handle that. She was consulting two patients simultaneously.

"Ma'am, I wanted to talk to you alone."

Just then, the lady who was sitting opposite to me opened her blouse and started showing her chest. It was really weird. I started looking at the other end of the room as if I had come there to watch the lunar eclipse.

The doctor wrote a couple of medicines for her with instructions. She instructed her in an authoritarian way, almost threatening her. Then she turned to me.

"Yes, tell me what the problem is."

"Ma'am, my wife is an HIV patient and she is pregnant. I wanted to know whether you have handled such cases in the past?"

Without even listening to me, she wrote something in complete Greek. Even an illiterate person could write better than her.

"Next patient!" she shouted.

Another lady who was almost inside the room settled in the opposite seat.

"Ma'am, I am not done with my explanation, how can you write a prescription?"

"These are tests – CD3 and CD4. Just conduct these tests and collect the report. Next time, come along with the patient. You may leave now."

"Next patient!" she screamed.

I stormed out in despair. This hospital was only for the brave and VVIPs. I thought about taking a look at the other facilities. CD4 and CD3 counts were especially used for AIDS patients. I decided to take a look at the labs in the hope of meeting some other patients who could guide me to another place.

After reaching the laboratory, I thanked my stars that there was no rush. Going closer I found that the lab was closed. One white chart was pasted on the closed door which said: 'Collect all reports between 4 to 5 p.m. Lunchtime – 1 to 2 p.m.'

I checked my watch and it showed 2.30. I found one old sickly man sitting in a terrible condition. I thought about asking him about it. "Uncle, why is it closed? Lunch time is already over."

Without even uttering a single word, he pointed his finger in the direction of a man, who was talking on his cell phone. I thought he might be the hospital's staff. I waited for him to finish his call. "Sir, why is this laboratory closed?" I enquired from the young man.

"Actually, they have gone for lunch."

"It is almost three."

"Sir, I am here with my patient," he pointed to the same old person and said, "You are in a government hospital."

This statement answered everything. People had to accommodate with this single excuse. Everyone had very little expectations from the government. I was still not sure of what to expect and what not to.

"How are you related to him?"

"He is my father."

"Is your father suffering from HIV?" I asked hesitantly. They were sitting outside the CD3 and the CD4 lab.

"Please don't say the word. Yes, my father is suffering from the same since the last one year," he whispered. I failed to understand why he did not want me to utter the name of the disease.

"Where do you come from?"

"Muzaffarnagar."

"Why did you come here all the way from Muzaffarnagar? Doesn't Muzaffarnagar have any hospitals?" I asked surprised.

"Actually sir, the moment our villagers came to know that my father is suffering from this, they threw us out. People stopped talking to us. We are just poor farmers. We have become untouchables for them, and were forced to leave that place." I instantly understood the reason behind his whispering. Till now, I had been fighting a medical problem, but now, I was handling a social issue.

"How long have you been here?"

"The past one month. Doctors have advised a strict medication plan and daily care."

"So, you are discharged?"

"No, he was never hospitalized. They said they did not have enough beds to accommodate us. We are staying nearby in a lodge in Mohammadpur and we come here every third day for treatment, tests, and medication. Facilities are poor here, but the doctors are very good," he said.

"How are the facilities poor?" I asked, not surprised this time.

"Sir, we've come here today the second time for CD4 and CD3 report. Yesterday the lab opened for only half the day as the lab staff was on leave."

"How is this possible? There wasn't a single staff person to give out the reports?"

"No, and today this person is still not back from his lunch break."

Suddenly, he saw someone coming and rose from his seat. "The pathologist has come."

I was still sitting and wondering if I should try a government hospital for Astha's treatment. I walked over to a nearby ward. I found that the patients were being mistreated more than being treated. Many patients were lying on the floor like neglected sick cows, craving for attention. Some of them were holding their own saline bottles in one hand while the other hand was being injected with it. It was difficult to imagine my wife being one of them. I moved back to question the pathologist.

Just as I was heading towards the cabin, the man I had met outside came out worried and started moving towards the exit.

"What happened?" I walked along with him.

"Sir, I have been asked to get certain things."

"What?" I said while walking along with him.

"They are out of pathology gloves and syringes. He instructed me to purchase these from outside."

"Wait, I am also coming with you. Does this happens every time?" I asked concerned.

"Yes, sir. Even if your patient is hospitalized, you have to purchase the medicines, syringes, consumables, gloves, cotton and all necessary things from outside."

"What kind of arrangement is this?"

"Sir, you are in a..." he started, but we said in unison, "government hospital!"

We purchased the gloves and started moving towards the lab. I fired another question.

"Do you know any HIV expert and economical doctors who are practicing outside, especially a gynaecologist?"

"There are a number of doctors you can find outside."

We reached the lab with the gloves, but the pathology staff came outside and said, "Sorry, you are late. It's 4.30 p.m."

"But you came back late from your lunch, doctor," I protested. He glared at me.

"Rules are rules and we are government servants."

He started walking down the corridor and said, "Come tomorrow."

"Tomorrow will never come, doctor," I shouted. It was the second time I had shouted at someone. Every person in the corridor stared at me.

The doctor ignored me and left in a hurry. I pitied that young man and his sick father. How they were running in circles since the last two days for a small test! If this was the condition of such a renowned metro hospital, what would be the condition of other small government hospitals? Only God knows.

The silence was broken by the man "Sir, I am leaving. So, how is your patient, which doctor are you consulting, here?" he asked concerned.

Meanwhile, I saw his father's eyes, the HIV patient who was running from Muzaffarnagar to Delhi. He was sitting on the floor, waiting for his imminent death. There was no life in his eyes; his thin skeleton, dark body and pathetic condition was unbearable. His will to live and fight back had been suppressed by our medical system.

"No, my wife will never be hospitalized here," I said clearly.

"Why sir?"

I said in affirmation, "Because this is a government hospital."

24

I could see a big storm brewing. It felt like an ocean of troubles, and I was going to drown in it. I was frustrated. I was going to be a father soon, but instead of being happy, I was sad. I was worried about my child's future.

In this situation, there was only one person who could help me out – my father. Astha's condition was stable for now, fortunately. We finished lunch together and when she proceeded for her noon nap, I decided to go and meet my father.

While I was driving, I remembered everything that had happened to me. I felt nothing more than a problematic child. At my age, everyone was doing something to make their parents proud. And then there I was – a liability. I felt worthless.

When I reached him, I told him about the discussion I had had with the doctor earlier. I wasn't able to speak while trying to control my emotions, but my father was a wise man who could read me like a book.

"Vijay, do not think about the negative things and focus on the things that you can do," he consoled. "What will be the amount?" My father was concerned, but I felt he was prepared for this.

"Around thirty lakhs."

He didn't look shocked.

"Don't worry son; we will arrange that money."

He looked confident. His confidence was enough to give me a sliver of hope.

"How are we going to do this, Papa?"

"That won't be a problem. We have this house. It may be twenty years old, but it's worth more than thirty lakhs."

He looked very calm during this conversation. All I could see was the love in his eyes and not a single ounce of regret.

He said with a smile, "After selling this house, we can move to a smaller apartment."

"This house belongs to both of you. I think you should ask mom before selling it. I don't think she will agree. At least not for Astha..."

"Do you think it's only about your wife? It's not for her, it's for you too. And she doesn't love anyone more than you. She will agree."

Helplessness and guilt started winning over me, again.

"Vijay, don't feel sorry. I know if you were in my place, you would have done the same."

That moment, I realized how lucky I was to have them stand by me, through thick and thin.

"Dad, I am such a disappointment. Don't you ever get frustrated with me?" .

"Why would I be frustrated? On the contrary, a son like you fills my heart with pride," he said with a fake smile.

"Dad, I don't deserve a father like you," I choked.

"You know, your only problem is underestimating yourself. You are a dutiful son."

"Dad, I know the truth," I said as he looked at me silently. I was blessed to have a supportive and understanding father like him. My father was a very wise man. His silence meant his next words would sort out my despair.

"Vijay, before you were born, I fought with your mom almost every single day. We decided to break apart, and then one day your mom gave me the best news of my life.

She had blessed me with a baby. I was never a happy man, neither with my job, nor with my wife. In my entire life, if I recall a happy moment, it is always related to you. So never feel sad or depressed because of the wrong reasons. You have given me everything, my son."

I didn't answer. All I could manage was a smile. A fake smile, struggling through tears. I don't know whether I was a good son or not, but I had the best father for sure.

"Forget that," he said, changing the topic, "what about the seven wishes that you are trying to accomplish?"

"Currently, I am focusing on her treatment. I don't think I can summon enough courage to fulfil her crazy wishes."

"But you should give it a try."

I nodded.

I prepared to leave because Astha was alone. He came out to see me off.

I fired my last question before starting my car.

"Papa, how are you going to manage the expenses? You may shift to some rented flat, but then your expenses will increase. I can be fired from my college job anytime now."

"Vijay, do you know the best part of retirement?"

"What?"

He gave a weird smile. "Pension."

25

I called Sargam and informed her about Astha's progress. To my surprise, Astha hadn't shared anything with her. It was strange as she only had Sargam as a friend. She informed me she would come to meet Astha on her birthday.

In the meantime, a different set of treatment started for Astha. Initially, she was not on drip, but after a few days, a lot of medicines were administered to her via IV. The hospital was taking care of her washing, cleaning and all her meals.

I was sitting on a chair, reading the newspaper, while Astha was sleeping. A nurse entered the ward. The nurse was completely covered, as if she had entered a gas chamber room, and even a minor exposure would harm her. She wore a blue-coloured coat, hand gloves and a mask. It was weird as she had only come to check her IV drip bottles. I noticed that Astha's fluid pipe had blood which was entering into the transparent pipe.

"Sister, there is blood in the fluid pipe."

"Ohh wait..." She went outside and called her junior to take care of it. They began a conversation in typical Hindi and Keralite accents.

"In private ward number seven, one patient expired."

"Ohh really sad." She sighed. "Every person has to pay the price of his action in this world itself," she said looking at Astha.

Astha was up by now and noticed them looking at her like that. I thought she would react; she was not the kind of girl who would listen to all those stupid things and digest. But this Astha was different. She ignored them.

After a few minutes, the doctor came for a routine check-up. I never discussed any detail in front of her. We'd go out and discuss the matter in detail. As usual, Astha asked little related to the baby or her recovery.

"How is Astha doing?" I asked.

"Till now, she is doing well, but her immunity is decreasing with every passing day. Somehow our medicines have been effective till now, but I am not sure what will happen next."

"Doctor, will this be a normal delivery or caesarian?" the question haunted me even in my sleep.

"I cannot say anything, but Astha is not in a position to deliver a baby normally," he sighed. "You already know what could be the worst part."

He kept his hand on my shoulder and said, "Hope for the best Vijay."

"When will the team of doctors be flying to India for Astha's case?"

"They will arrive in fifteen days. They are assessing her reports on a daily basis. I am in regular touch with them."

●

Papa was the only one who came to visit her in the hospital. As usual, mom refused to visit her. I did not inform my colleagues deliberately. I had to hide her disease. After all, I was struggling with a social problem too. A few more days passed. Astha's due date was only a few weeks away. I had mixed feelings churning inside me. I was amazed that I had successfully managed to hide her disease from her, but worried at same time as to how I'd inform her. Her birthday was round the corner too. It could be her last birthday; it had to be grand, I thought.

"You want a gift for your birthday?" I couldn't resist asking her.

"No, I already have the best gift. A loving husband and my baby," she said with contentment and touched her baby bump. "I will celebrate a grand birthday next year with the baby." There was life in her eyes.

I wouldn't let her leave me at any cost, no matter what. Her negligent dreams gave me a reason to fight.

"Why do you want to wait for the next year to celebrate a grand birthday?"

"Vijay, I don't want any gift, no formality."

"Who said I am giving you a grand gift?" I teased her.

"Vijay, why are you not going to college regularly? I am fine and can manage everything on my own."

"You don't worry about that," I said caressing her forehead.

"Vijay, please understand. I am a normal patient, and the doctors and nurses are here to take care of me. You need to go to college regularly."

"I will go once you are okay."

"No Vijay, your principal had called you for the college event, you have to assist him. I know the event is on my birthday, but still you have to be there."

"It's a promise... I will not miss the event after the baby is here."

"After the baby, everything will change."

"Really! How?"

"After the baby, we will be threesome awesome. I will have one more person to talk to. You rarely talk." She changed the topic.

"You will only talk?"

"No, we will party. You have been promoted to professor; I am sure after some time you will be promoted to HOD, and we will be a rich family. Whenever you go for your college outing, we will go on our own outing. We will roam around in the city in our car."

"But an HOD never goes for an outing," I said for the lack of anything better to say.

"That is excellent. Then we can all go out together," she said. Each word was piercing my heart since I was the one who knew what the truth was. "Vijay, I want a commitment from you."

"What kind of commitment?"

"Vijay, I know as a human being you are the best person, but I want to see a confident person in you. I want you to be a fearless person."

"How can I prove it?"

"You will face things that scare you the most. Kill your fears, Vijay. Kill them and become a confident man."

"I will try."

"Seeing a husband rising in his career and becoming a confident person is the best gift of life."

I promised myself I will prove her right. I will give her the best gift of life.

26

Astha's condition had worsened. She often vomited and required assistance for doing almost every task. Her legs and back ached, and her weight was not increasing the way it was supposed to. It was not surprising, but difficult to accept.

It was her birthday, and also the college annual function. I was the first to wish her, on probably her last birthday. Sargam was there, and Astha was happy she had a visitor with whom she could talk and share some happy moments. Sargam's presence had changed the air in the ward. Sargam gave me my Astha back. After so many days, she was laughing.

The doctor came in and we came out for a discussion. This time, Sargam also came along.

"Listen, Vijay, the baby is growing a bit faster than we anticipated; we may have to operate Astha before the due date."

"So, a normal delivery will not be an option?"

"You can discuss this matter with Dr Rachna, but I feel it will most probably be a caesarian child. Astha doesn't have enough strength to go for a normal delivery."

I didn't reply. My eyes were tearing up. Sargam asked a few questions. Those were the same questions that I had asked many times before.

"Vijay, take care and be brave," the doctor said.

As the doctor left, Sargam and I planned a few things for Astha's birthday surprise.

We entered the room.

"Listen, guys, you sit and talk. I have to go to college for the function."

"Are you sure you are going to college?" Astha asked. "Why?"

"Your principal called you for the preparations. You missed all that, and now you are going directly to the function. Your principal will kill you."

"Who cares?" I said confidently.

●

It was a day of celebration for Sri Ram College of Art, Sciences and Commerce. For this day, the entire college had worked for a full year. Almost five thousand students were waiting to showcase their talent. Girls were displaying their rare fashion skills, and as usual, boys were craving for hot chicks. But we the teachers had to behave like a government; everything happens in front of us, but we can only take action if it is official. The smaller events normally took place in our auditorium, but since this was the annual function, a lot of guests had been invited from outside. Many HR professionals, senior corporate leaders, some ex-alumni and every person who was associated with the college was invited. Considering the high turn up, it was not possible for the auditorium to accommodate five thousand guests. A big tent had been set up for the occasion; many sponsors were arranged, and media persons were invited.

Live telecast was scheduled on the Campus Channel. *The Spark* magazine was publishing only about the festival for the last couple of months. I chose a corner seat. It was my bad luck since the principal saw me and he waved his hand to call me.

"Good afternoon sir," I said approaching him.

"Good afternoon my dear chief guest. So, how is the arrangement? Hope you are enjoying every bit of it," he mocked.

"It is good."

"Really, thank you so much for your kind words."

"Sir, I am sorry I couldn't help. My wife is really unwell."

"Oh I know, you are expecting a baby." I didn't answer. I wanted him to vomit out all his frustration. "It was my biggest mistake to appoint you as a faculty in my college."

"Sorry sir."

"Get lost!" He raised his voice before going to his seat.

After the inauguration ceremony, the event finally started with the first competition. A couple of cameras were capturing the event from various angles.

I was sitting in my agony, wondering how my father was so happy about my joining the college. Never did I reveal that I was just an assistant professor who rarely taught the students when my family projected me as a senior professor while hunting for a bride. In the last few hours, I had been thinking, how tough it is for a person, who stands there and faces a crowd of five thousand. Lunch break was announced for half an hour; the rest of the events were to resume at 2.30 p.m. I opened the sheet in which Astha had written down her weird wishes. It read: *"Seven impossible wishes before I die"*.

Around 2.30 p.m., the principal was back with the chief guest and the audience was already settled, but the camera was off. The show was about to start. I sent a text to Sargam and then I went up to the girl who was anchoring the event.

"Listen, dear, I have to make an announcement."

"Announcement? Sir, you cannot make any announcement, the camera is about to be switched on and will start broadcasting. Our chief guest is here."

"It is an important announcement. I have the principal's permission." Since my name was still up as the event in-charge in some papers, she did not protest.

She signalled the camera person to keep the recording off for the while. I went straight to the mike, and for the first time in my life faced five thousand people. Every eye was glaring, clearly irritated with the delay in the programme. The principal looked like he'd swallow me in the next couple of seconds. I was unaffected. I knew what I had to say. The man who had faltered in front of five panelists was facing a crowd of five thousand.

"Dear friends, good evening." No one responded. "Friends, I am working here as an assistant professor of English. Most of you know me." I found it very difficult to speak; I was shivering, literally. The presence of the chief guest forced the principal to behave nicely, but he looked like he was going to explode in anger. He stood up from his seat and instructed the camera person to shut down the camera.

"Friends, I haven't come here for the function. I have come here as a husband."

The crowd sniggered.

"I was married about eleven months back and today my wife is hospitalized. She is pregnant, and if God blesses us, we may have a healthy child. But…but I don't know whether she will be alive to see that day or not." I had a lump in my throat. The audience went completely silent. I knew I had their attention now.

"She is suffering from a fatal disease and the doctors have confirmed that the end is not very far. The next year, when you all will be celebrating this annual festival, Astha, my wife will not be alive to see this." I pulled out my handkerchief and dabbed my eyes. There was pin drop silence.

"Sorry for dragging you all into this, but today I am celebrating her twenty-eighth birthday. She has been hospitalized for the last few weeks and according to the doctors, she has limited days to live. I am an ordinary man. My wife always had a desire to have a grand birthday party. I asked her what the meaning of a grand birthday was. According to her, thousands of people wishing her on her birthday and singing a song for her would be grand."

I fixed my gaze at the principal. He was staring at me with his piercing eyes and holding the camera guy.

"I am a poor person and not in a position to host a party for so many people. I would be grateful if you can wish her a happy birthday. I am sure she will be watching it from a distance." But the principal was unmoved. "I want to thank my principal for giving me a chance to stand here and use this platform." He did not move.

"Friends, can you help me fulfil her grand birthday wish."

My eyes were dripping wet by now. One lady from the crowd stood up and started clapping. "Wish you a very happy birthday Astha."

A couple of girls followed. And after a few seconds, five thousand voices chorused the birthday song in a rhythm. I looked at the principal. He didn't know what to do.

The camera person switched on the camera, and captured live all the people standing and singing the birthday song.

"Happy birthday to you, happy birthday dear Astha, may God bless you, may you have a long life, happy birthday to you..."

A few kilometres away from the college, in a hospital ward, Sargam and Astha watched this live.

After the event, I laughed like a crazy man and mumbled, "Astha, my score is two out of seven."

27

The principal might have killed me if I would have stayed there for another minute. I had spoiled his college function, and he was certainly mad at me. I came out and headed straight for Noida. The presence of Sargam with Astha had given me additional time to arrange certain things. I went to meet my best friend, my father. No sooner had he opened the door, I clung to his chest and embraced him tightly.

"What's wrong Vijay?" he had sensed the emotions in the tight hug.

"I have good news." I brightened.

"Great! What brings this bemused smile on your face? Nowadays I am even scared of your happiness." His sarcasm made us both laugh.

"I have fulfiled one more wish." I said and described the events. He was amazed and delighted at the same time. The heart of a father cannot be prouder when hearing the stories of the accomplishments of his children.

"You really did that! We must celebrate her birthday better than ever." I sensed a strange happiness in his voice. He went to the kitchen and came back with a box of coconut barfi. He took out a big piece and stuffed it into my mouth. It was a big moment for me. It had been very long since he had done this. The last time he fed me a sweet was when I had cleared the written exam for PCS.

"That's my boy." He was mad with happiness and proud at the same time.

"Papa, I think it's high time I talk to her about her disease."

"Why? Why now?"

"There are only eighteen days to go for her operation, and you know what that means."

"What good do you expect to come out of it?"

"Papa, Astha is extremely confident about the future. She goes on about our life after the baby. Buying a new home, sending our child to a school and lots of other stuff. I don't want her dreams to be shattered just like that in a second. She will not be alive to see all these things. I don't know how she will react."

"Astha is a mature girl; she will understand."

"Papa, if suddenly she gets to know that she will not be alive in the next few days and that all her dreams are going to come to naught, expecting her to act mature is childish."

I had talked to my father like that for the first time. "Papa, I am fed up of lying to her," I said in tears. I had become a person who cried very often. "Papa, every day when I see her inspiring eyes, I see her wish to see her baby grow old."

"Vijay, you have fought everything so bravely; you cannot become weak at this point now."

"How am I supposed to tell her the truth now? Papa, can you do it for me?"

"There's no way in the world anyone can understand this. Accepting certain death and being at peace with it is something even the most enlightened saints lack." I didn't understand what he was saying.

"Vijay, please try to understand, you don't need to tell her anything." I was inconsolable, but what he said next shook me. "She already knows everything."

"What!" I said shocked. I couldn't believe it.

She knew that she was dying, but she had still played along with me for so long.

"She is aware that she is suffering from HIV."

"So you told her?"

"Please don't get me wrong, my son."

"For how long has she been aware of this?"

"The last five months."

"Why did you do this and why didn't you inform me about this?" I demanded an answer from my father.

"Vijay, Astha had figured this out herself and called me to confirm. A pregnant mother who is HIV positive requires all the care. You cannot be available all the time."

So for the last few months, I was under the impression that I was hiding this fact from her. But she was the one faking a smile like a doll. Suddenly everything started to make sense – why Astha had begun to behave differently and why she didn't ask questions. How my egoistic lady had left everything behind and started talking like a saint.

"But you could have told me about that," I asked in agony.

"It was her wish, beta."

•

Papa gave me a cheque of ten lakhs as the first deposit for the treatment. I was laden with guilt as I headed towards the hospital.

"Hey, where have you been?"

"Sorry for the delay, I went to meet Papa. When did Sargam leave?"

"She just left, and why did you do that? You may get sacked." I ignored her comment.

"It's okay Astha. I am thinking of the baby. After the baby, we shall shift to Noida with my parents."

I avoided eye contact. It was hard to face her.

"You know, I was also thinking the same thing. The presence of elders helps in nurturing a baby. On the one hand, your father will be telling all his stories related to crime, and on the other hand, your journalist mother will spin stories of celebrities. You will teach him English since you didn't teach anything in college. At least, you can brush up your skills on the baby."

How could she smile in such a condition? Her words broke the dam of tears that I had been holding for so many minutes. She noticed my tears.

"Why are you... So Papa told you everything?" She guessed correctly.

"Astha, you are an excellent actor. How can you act like this? How…." I said and hugged her and started weeping like a child. I kept mumbling, "Why did you get the infection Astha, why? You cannot do this to me."

I had wanted to hug her and cry for the last five months. In spite of the tears in our eyes, I felt relieved. Even in that condition, she replied: *"Always try to represent yourself as 'happy', because one day it becomes your personality."*

28

"Vijay, the situation is changing at a tremendous pace. It's likely that we will have to operate within ten days," Dr Raza answered the biggest question of my life.

Dr Raza was aware that Astha had been informed officially about her ailment and the consequences of a caesarian delivery. After having handled Astha's case for months now, Dr Raza and Dr Rachna were personally involved in many of my decisions.

The hospital informed me of the unpaid dues. I had already broken my bank, but hospitals don't care. They are the best in slipping the bills with ease to a patient. Everyday, Dr Raza came in and we discussed the progress and the next course of action. The patient was spared the agony of it as he insisted on getting it all done in private.

"What about the visiting doctors who were supposed to be here by now."

"They have already boarded the flight. They'll be here by tomorrow. Vijay, not only are they doctors, but also scientists devoted to the cause of finding a cure for AIDS."

"Oh great! But are you very sure that Astha cannot have a normal delivery?"

"Vijay, I want you to understand very clearly that Astha is not doing very well. Her amino acids level and CD4 counts are further reducing. I am sure that she will need a caesarian delivery. Let's keep our fingers crossed and hope for the best."

Whenever I lost hope, something always came as a light in the darkness. This time, it was in the form of scientists and doctors from the USA.

●

Astha had gained a few kilos, but had become fragile; it was difficult for her to even breathe. Her legs, body, lungs, and joints began to hurt. To sum it up, she was completely immersed in grief.

I often sat by her side and pressed her legs, and stroked her head with my hands. Astha's weakness was a big reason to worry, but it was not the only problem I had. Since my love was struggling for her life, the rest of the problems were the least of my concerns.

A team of three doctors arrived for the US the very next day. Including the Indian doctors, a total of half a dozen people were working on her case. I still remember the days very clearly, when I was chasing the nurses to get her treated. And now, here I was, with a whole bunch of doctors trying to find the best strategy to keep her alive. Doctors spent half an hour in the ward. They examined her thoroughly and added a couple of tests to the to-do list.

I was keen to know their conclusion and the best way to move forward. However, they insisted on talking after they had the results with them.

I was called in the next day. The same team of half a dozen doctors including Dr Rachna was there, ready for me.

"Hi Vijay," they chorused in unison.

"Hello doctors. Thank you for all your efforts."

"Oh, don't be so formal," said one of the doctors in an impeccable American accent.

"How is Astha? Is she doing well? What about her due date? Is there any chance of a healthy delivery?" I wanted a lot of answers.

"Vijay, we cannot guarantee anything. We still have around ten days for the normal delivery, unless she develops any severe pain indicating a complication."

"What are her chances of survival if she goes for a caesarian delivery?" It was tough to hear them answer my question, but I had to ask.

"It would be tough for her to recover after she undergoes an operation." Another American doctor said. "The patient has become weak; it's difficult to ensure even the safety of the baby at this stage."

"But according to Dr Raza, she is not doing that bad," I said looking at Dr Raza.

"Vijay, the way the results of her tests are fluctuating, we cannot assure you of anything. It can go either side."

"Doctor, I want to state one thing very clearly. My prime focus is Astha, and I expect you to bring her back. Anyhow… even if it means that we lose our baby." That was one thing I was certain of.

They nodded.

"Vijay, our prime focus is on the case, and it includes both the mother and the child. Recently, an Australian scientist has developed a medicine that is very useful for pregnant women. In some cases, it is found that this drug is very effective in delivering an HIV-negative child even from an active mother."

"So start giving her those medicines. What is the problem?"

"Those medicines have some side effects. We are administering small doses to her, to check her body's response. These antibiotics can help to protect your baby from this disease and can also give strength to Astha. Just that those antibiotics are not yet commercialized and are very expensive."

"How much?"

"Two-and-a-half thousand dollars," answered one doctor. I was not sure about the exact conversion, but I multiplied the amount with INR seventy to get an approximate idea."

It was close to two lakhs. I could manage that.

"Please go ahead." I said with some ray of hope.

"Vijay, it's the amount per day."

"What!" There was pin drop silence in the room. My mind did some mental calculations. She had to go through this treatment for the next nine days or so. I had to manage another eighteen lakhs.

Would I be able to do that?

•

I came back to the ward and found Astha with Sargam. When no one even dared to touch her, Sargam sat on her bed, and soothed her without hesitation or fear of any kind. Sargam was a true friend.

When I sat with them, they mocked me and narrated their boozing stories as if they deserved a Nobel peace prize for that. They were talking and giggling away, so I went to the hospital's cafeteria and ordered a coffee. I needed it badly. The sudden increase in the cost had become impossible to manage. I wondered why I had never cared to get a health insurance. I hated myself for it.

I took the last corner seat. I was lost in my agony, thinking of ways to arrange for the funds when I saw a lady coming out of an auto. I knew her very well. She enquired something at the reception and moved towards the lift. I ran to meet her. We both entered the lift together.

"Mom, you are here! I asked shocked, but my mother didn't answer. The presence of two unknown people in the lift didn't allow us to start the conversation. We reached the fifth floor.

"Are you here to meet Astha?" I asked outside the lift.

"No, I have come here to meet my daughter-in-law."

"Mom, how did this miracle happen?"

"A boy who never had the courage to speak even in front of a single person dared to speak in front of five thousand people without caring about his job. Don't you think that's a miracle?"

"Oh, the principal complained, I guess," I said indifferently.

"Can I see her?"

"Mom, you cannot meet her."

"Why?"

"She doesn't want to meet anybody who pities her."

"You don't worry Vijay. She is not just your responsibility." She smiled, "Do you remember the last time when you said 'no' to me for anything."

"I didn't get you, mom."

"Vijay, I am your mother, and you have never confronted me with anything since your childhood. You had never been a decision maker." She passed a strange smile and said, "Beta, everything has changed."

29

From Vijay's Mother

I am Vijay's mom. I think it's better to share my version of the story for a better perspective, else this father and son duo will write just anything. I met Vijay's father during his initial days of service. He was a much-decorated police officer. We were poles apart in every aspect, but his honesty attracted me. I always knew that it would be difficult, but then I asked myself which relationship is perfect? We took our chances and got married.

But as time passed, Vijay was the only link that kept our relationship going. Loving Vijay and looking after him were the only things we did in common. I wanted him to be an engineer, but his father wanted him to be an IAS officer.

Vijay was a good child; he never opposed anything. Generally, his father wasn't home, so I was a bit strict with him. Vijay was my only responsibility. He was always a mamma's boy. His father visited home occasionally, so he always brought him something and never forced him to study. I gradually turned out to be a villain in his dictionary and as time passed, Vijay became closer to his father. They started to spend more and more time with each other. I was never too comfortable with all this, but somewhere I knew I was responsible.

My over expectations spoiled Vijay. He turned into a disaster, and his confidence crashed, making him feel useless.

One day, Vijay was sitting inside his room weeping. Vijay was crying because he had failed to clear the written exam for the IAS, fifth time in a row.

I decided to help him. Being a journalist, I had relations with the college principal and requested him to find a spot for Vijay in Sriram College. Finally, Vijay got a job. But he wasn't made for that, and it was a disaster too. His principal always complained that Vijay rarely taught the classes. I pleaded, and the chief gave him non-academic work in college.

We decided to find him a wife. A herculean task for a mother whose child keeps his mouth shut. He was an above average looking guy. We met more than a dozen girls, but each one of them said no. No girl wanted to spend her life with an introvert Mumma's boy.

I lied that Vijay was a bright, intelligent PCS aspirant. After all, a mother never thinks twice before compromising for her husband or children.

Finally, we met Astha. I could never understand why a girl like Astha had agreed to marry Vijay. But we were happy.

Astha was not a perfect match for Vijay. To be frank, she wasn't even a match in any way. They were mirror opposites of each other. Vijay was an introvert, and Astha was an extrovert. Her favourite dishes were non-vegetarian, and she even boozed at times.

Did you think I would tolerate all this? I could have, but it was later uncovered that Astha was an illegitimate child. A street rubbish married to my only son. No, that wasn't happening. I decided to throw her out. One beautiful day, the smell of an omelette spreading through the house served as a tipping point to execute the decision.

She was a foxy lady; she played with Vijay's mind. She magically hypnotized Vijay overnight. He turned into a puppet, a henpecked husband. Vijay never spoke a word against Astha.

He decided to move out to a rented apartment near her office. At last, Astha and Vijay moved out of our home.

My happy family broke. I didn't have a reason to stay at home, and I started taking assignments for outdoor events. My baby, my only love had shifted to Malviya Nagar. I hated Astha from the bottom of my soul.

But when I returned from South Africa, everything had changed. Astha was prègnant. I was jubilant, but the irony was that my jealousy for Astha did not even allow me to congratulate her. I met Vijay on his birthday. Vijay was not the same person anymore; he was different. Frankly speaking, I hated this change in him, but couldn't deny this change was good.

Vijay's father came to me with papers to mortgage our flat. I discovered that Astha was suffering from HIV. I enquired how she got the infection, but technically and medically, no once could diagnose the reason. My heart sank. She would take Vijay down with her.

It is hard to believe, but I was relieved when I found Vijay was safe. His father told me how Vijay was trying to fulfil her stupid wishes. I hated her crazy wishes, but I was happy that Vijay had decided to take a stand and fight for something.

Vijay's principal informed me of his declaration in the college event. The principal who never said anything positive about Vijay ended up appreciating him. My heart went out for my son; I had tears in my eyes. A person who could not even open his mouth in front of a girl, had managed to speak in front of five thousand people…in front of a live camera.

I forgave Astha because she had given me something that only a mother could understand. The girl had transformed my son. I decided to try to fulfil all her secret wishes. I decided to meet my daughter-in-law. After all, she had given me a confident son.

30

From Vijay's Mother II

I *went into the ward, and took them by surprise. Sargam was sitting beside Astha. She greeted me, and I instantly recognized her from the drinking incident in my home. Sargam pretended to have got a call and left the room. I guess she wasn't comfortable with me. There were just the two of us left inside that room.*

Astha had become dull; it was difficult to believe that she was the same girl who was always full of joy. Her face had lost its charm. I never really liked her, but seeing her like that made me hate myself.

"Hi Astha! How are you beta?" I asked. "Don't get up; it's alright." I put my hand on her shoulder. "How are you feeling?" After hating her for all those years, the guilt crept in.

"I am good, Mom. I am glad and a little surprised to see you here."

"I came to meet my daughter. How can this be a surprise?" My heart was heavy. She tried to fake a smile. She looked good when she smiled.

"I see everything has changed now," she said.

"I am going to be a grandmother soon, so I decided to meet you."

She seemed to have taken my words otherwise.

"Mom, I don't need any sympathy. I understand that my days are numbered, but I am still happy," she said.

"Beta, who said I want to sympathize? I just want to thank you." I was in a tough spot.

"I am the reason your son does not live with you. I am the reason that you had to sell your house," she said without any emotion. "I should be thankful to you for helping me. I owe everything that I am to you and your family."

"Astha, don't think like this, my child. We are family. We've had our differences in the past, but you have done what I never could do. You have made my son responsible. He is now more confident and mature than he ever was. He is no more a helpless man."

She didn't say anything, so I continued, "By the way, belated happy birthday. I have brought a few presents for you." I handed her a pink shawl and took out the cake I had brought for her.

"Is this an eggless cake?" she asked jokingly.

I laughed. We talked for an hour. I could see that it was difficult for her to talk, but still she didn't want to stop even for a minute. She told me everything about the past few days. I felt different with her this time. I knew that I would be the one to nurture the child. It was after a long time that we didn't fight and talked like normal adults. I behaved like a caring mother whose daughter was due to deliver a baby in a few days.

"Please take good care of yourself, beta. I will leave now," I got up from my seat.

"Mom, I have a request. Please don't get me wrong."

"Sure dear. What is it?"

"You know that I cannot be cured and would be gone very soon."

"Please don't talk like that."

"Mom, let's accept the truth. I don't want to see my loved ones standing in front of me with eyes full of tears. I don't

want all those people around whose presence is going to make me weak." Her nose turned pink and her eyes were full of tears.

"You are a brave girl, beta. You cannot lose hope." I was standing there helpless. I could not do anything to help her, and I could only lie.

"Mom, I don't have much time now, and I don't want to see anyone getting hurt. It makes me weak. Please don't come to see me again."

That was the strong girl I knew and I had always respected her for that.

"I will honour your wish." I picked up my bag, and it felt like the last interaction with my daughter-in-law whom I had just discovered. I wanted to say something more, but before I could say anything, Astha said, *"Thank you, mom, for giving me a husband like him. I am sorry for all the trouble I have caused you."* We were both in tears. I tried to ignore her apology and tried to tell her what I really felt.

"Astha, I have always criticized you and insulted you because you were an illegitimate child. But now I realize that no child is illegitimate. They are not responsible for that." I took a deep breath. *"I know it will be a little weird, but I never gave you a hug. I want to do it now. Can I hug you?"*

With tears in her eyes, she nodded her head.

I hugged her, and I had nothing but love for her. The best memory I have had with her in all those years. I hugged my Astha, my daughter, for the first and last time and cried in silence.

"I am sorry, beta. I am very sorry."

I wanted to tell her how sorry I was, and all I wanted was her to be happy.

"I never knew what it's like to have a mother. My stepmother never hugged me. She didn't care. My pillow was

the only mother I had. But today, I've found my mother. Thank you for letting me know how it feels to have a mother before I go. I love you Mom."

"Love you too," I replied with teary eyes.

There was a deafening silence in the room. I started walking towards the door. She waved and tried to smile. I could see how miserable she was feeling, but she was putting up one hell of a fight.

"Vijay is not the only one who has changed; you too have changed."

31

Mom had a discussion with Dr Raza to understand Astha's condition. She was concerned about her. She asked everything, about her disease, her condition and the further cost of her treatment. Now I knew I had one more shoulder to let me through this difficult period. Sargam was there to take care of Astha, so I decided to drop Mom home.

I had no money left with me, and this problem demanded immediate attention. We left for home. There was silence inside the car. I knew my mother well; there was something going on in her mind, and I chose to keep quiet. I could guess the reason for her behaviour. Finally, we reached home. It was locked from the outside.

"Where is Dad?" I asked my mother. My father was a retired man, and he was not someone who leaves home without any reason. She didn't say a word and took out the keys from her purse.

"You don't know? That's strange," she said. "I thought he only keeps things from me. Anyway, he will be here in a few minutes. You can ask him." Any discussion about him always ended like that.

We had tea. I felt that I had no idea about the sacrifices a woman makes in her life before this day. I was looking at a woman, who despite being emotionally drained out did her job, handled her wasted marriage every day, looked at her useless son and even then chose to be silent. I was seeing things more clearly now, being a husband as well as a son. My thoughts were interrupted after fifteen minutes when Dad arrived. He carried a bag. I asked him about his whereabouts and he ignored me.

"Who is with Astha?" he asked

"Sargam," I answered.

I told him about Mom's visit to the hospital and her chat with Dr Raza. Finally, I told him about the money requirements.

"Additional two lakhs per day!" he exclaimed.

"Vijay, there is something you need to know." He was calm, but I could sense that something wasn't right. "I had incorrectly anticipated the worth of this house. It's a twenty-five-year-old property, and I can't find a buyer to pay us over twenty lakhs. I have already given you ten lakhs and have another ten that you can take whenever you want." He sipped the tea served by Mom.

"Sanjay, the total expense of the medical costs would range somewhere around forty-five, including everything, right?" my mother asked.

"Yes, treatment in a private hospital is very expensive."

"Can we talk to our relatives?"

"I can't think of anyone who can lend us this big an amount?" Dad said.

"What about your jewellery?" he asked.

"Ha-ha. Right!" she laughed sarcastically. "If you remember, ours was a love marriage, and I hope you remember the circumstances in which we got married. I could never purchase anything in the name of jewellery for myself," Mom replied.

It was the first time they talked about their marriage in front of me. The last time they had discussed something like this was when the tenth girl had rejected my marriage proposal. It was kind of amazing to see how a problem can unite a family.

"Vijay, do you know anyone who can help us in getting a loan?" Dad asked.

"I know one of Astha's friends, Daniel." That's the only name that came to my mind.

"Vijay, the bank never gives a loan to a person who does not have any security to give," Mom said while rejecting the option.

"What about the principal of your college? You can ask for a personal loan from your college," my father suggested.

"I don't think so. I am not even sure if he would let me continue with the job," I said.

Suddenly, my mom got up and said, "Excuse me. I have to submit an article."

Sometimes I wonder why my mom always gives so much importance to her work. It was kind of weird for me, given the matter at hand.

Was she the same person who had cried for Astha a few hours ago?

32

Five lakh rupees were deposited to the hospital, and a sum of a few more lakhs was kept reserved for an emergency. This installment gave me a few days to arrange for the next massive amount. There was no ego, no hesitation, and surprisingly no fear. I was ready to beg anyone who could help me with the money.

After my declaration in college, many of my colleagues and relatives got to know about Astha's illness. However, they were still unaware of her HIV condition. Astha refused to meet anyone. She had her reasons, and I respected that. Sargam was the only one who was allowed to meet her. Sargam came to the hospital in the evening every day and stayed until nightfall. Together, they seemed different. I was fascinated, maybe because I never had a true friend in my life. A friend would have been great for support through all this.

A couple of days later, Astha developed problems in breathing. I discussed it with the doctors, and they suggested using an oxygen mask on SOS basis. According to them, it was not a big concern. The situation was at a standstill: neither was she doing well nor was she deteriorating further. I had lots to ponder upon. But Astha's terminal disease had made every other problem trivial. The loud ringtone of my phone brought me back into the current world.

"Hi, Papa. How are you?"

"How is Astha?" Papa asked. These days everyone who called had a common question, and I had the same answer to repeat.

"The fight is on, and the situation is under control."

"Vijay, what is the score?"

"Score? I didn't get you?"

"Remember, her seven wishes?"

"Yes, I do remember her seven crazy wishes, but why are you asking?" I was not at all concerned about her wishes. How to manage the expenses was the biggest challenge for me.

"Did you happen to read the latest publication of your college magazine?" His voice had an enthusiasm which was rare.

"No, I haven't. What happened?"

"First have a look at that, and remember, everything is possible if we believe in it." He disconnected the call mysteriously. It was an unusual call. First, he never had a habit of reading anything, second, where did he manage a subscription copy of the magazine? Third, how can her crazy wishes be related to it? I had to find out.

I unlocked my messy house after six days. It was awful for me to see my house in that condition. Only a lady can turn a house into a home. When Astha was here, it was a different place altogether. I found newspapers and magazines lying on the ground, unattended. There were two magazines the courier guy must have slipped under the door. I picked up both. One was the regular health magazine and the second was the college's annual publication.

"No, this is not possible!" I screamed.

I stared at my college magazine. I went numb, and it was unbelievable for me. The front cover of my college magazine had a full picture of my wife. She looked young and beautiful. For a moment, I sympathized about her current look. She had lost her beauty.

Questions teemed inside my head. Why did the college not display a photo of their recent event? How did they get her picture? Who had given them the permission to tell her story openly? Why did my college not inform me about this? Was it a trick played by the principal? How come Papa got to know about this first? What could be the motive behind this? How will Astha react when she comes to know? Was Astha already aware of this?

Below Astha's photo was a line in bold fonts which read:

A truly inspiring and eye-opening story of a pregnant HIV positive woman – Page-16

●

Hi, I am Astha. I am an HIV patient. I thought I should tell my story to people. Just imagine, what comes to your mind when you hear about someone who is infected with HIV? I am not generalizing everyone, but people think an AIDS patient is a sex worker or an immoral person. Before saying anything else or even formulating an opinion, I want you to read on:

In a school in Goa, thirteen orphans are suffering from AIDS. These students were expelled because other parents complained to school authorities. The parents also asked the school to expel the other twenty-three orphans although they were not HIV-positive.

It was not just this school which showed them the door. After their expulsion, these students were moved to a boarding school run by Salesian priests in Sulcorna, twelve kilometres away from Rivona. But after six days, this school too asked the child home to withdraw the children, saying they were facing problems from some parents.

Finally, these thirteen students were shifted to a school in North Goa. After facing flak from various organizations, the school decided not to expel the other twenty-three orphans from their school.

The children are aged between six to fifteen years.

Do you think all these kids are sex workers? Are we living in a society where Gandhi Ji taught us to hate the sin, not the sinner? Can anyone say these kids are immoral?

- *An estimated 33.4 million people worldwide were living with HIV (2008).*
- *Approximately 2.1 million children under fifteen were living with HIV (2007).*

The day I was diagnosed positive for HIV, I wondered how I got the disease. My husband was the first one who came to know about my infection.

My liver got infected, and the doctor suggested a full-time nurse at home. No nurse was ready to work for me. Even more surprising was that many doctors were not ready to treat me. In the hospital, I found that nurses refused to touch me. They wore face masks and gloves all the time while around me. They were always equipped with extra protection, especially when entering my room. Sometimes I felt like an untouchable. For the last six months, what we have faced is even worse than being infected.

AIDS is often seen as 'someone else's problem'. Even as it moves into the general population, the HIV epidemic is still misunderstood by Indians. People living with HIV have faced violent attacks, been rejected by families, spouses and communities, been refused medical treatment, and even in some reported cases, denied the last rites after death.

I am not a doctor, and I have no authority to teach anyone anything, but day I got to know about the infection, I went through many journals. After all, I am a victim, and it's my moral responsibility to give courage to all other people who are fighting physically, and mentally, against a disease that is not even their fault.

Here are some lesser known reasons for HIV:

- *Being born to an infected mother. HIV can be passed from mother to child during pregnancy, birth, or breastfeeding.*
- *Being stuck with an HIV-contaminated needle or a sharp object.*
- *Receiving blood transfusions, blood products, or organ/tissue transplants that are contaminated with HIV.*
- *Eating food that has been pre-chewed by an HIV-infected person. The contamination occurs when infected blood from a patient's mouth mixes with food while chewing.*
- *Being bitten by a person with HIV. There is no risk of transmission if the skin is not broken.*
- *Contact between broken skin, wounds, or mucous membranes and HIV-infected blood or blood-contaminated body fluids.*
- *Deep, open-mouth kissing if the person with HIV has sores or bleeding gums and blood is exchanged.*

HIV is NOT spread by:
- *Air or water*
- *Insects, including mosquitoes or ticks*
- *Saliva, tears, or sweat*
- *Casual contact, like shaking hands, hugging or sharing dishes/drinking glasses*

An AIDS patient goes through double the trauma. First, they have to prove themselves innocent. It's something that they are unable to do in their lifetime; second, they have to fight the disease.

Let me tell you that my husband never asked about the source of my infection. He loves me. He was incapable of affording the best treatment, but he did not leave any stone unturned and made it possible.

I am not telling you my story because I want sympathy. Today, I am confident in sharing the truth so openly because of the love I have received from my husband and family. It doesn't matter how deadly the disease is if you have people who love you, believe in you – it changes the battle completely.

Imagine a society where AIDS patients are not sacked from offices. They are not thrown out of a rented home; they are not sacked from the school or any social community. People have no problem in hugging them or shaking hands with them. Every doctor and nurse is eager to help in their treatment.

Doctors say that a stable AIDS patient can live like a normal person for more than ten to fifteen years, if well-cared for. A ten-year life filled with love cannot be compared to anything in this world, not even a hundred-year life. We can defeat every disease by finding the cure, and giving unmatched love.

Today I am pregnant, and I don't know whether my child will or won't be affected with this virus. Being a mother, I have a humble request. If he or she turns out to be an HIV patient, please do not treat him or her as an untouchable. My child will not be responsible for the disease. My child doesn't want your sympathy. He or she only deserves your love.

There is no sin, and I am not a sinner.
An AIDS patient is just a patient.

–Written and edited by Sushma Sharma

33

After the article got published, people were lining up to meet Astha. Many of my colleagues and friends were eager to talk to her. A few months ago, I was struggling all alone, and now there were so many people eager to take care of her. A few of them offered financial help, but forty-five lakhs was still too much.

After a few days, I got a call from the accounts department of the hospital. My credit limit was about to get exhausted. I went to the accounts department and requested them to give me a few extra days to arrange the money. They agreed to give me an extension.

Dr Raza was my only way out of this. Next morning, I waited eagerly for him to come for his round.

"Doctor, can we shift Astha to a general ward?" I asked.

"Why, what happened?"

"Doctor, you know our situation well. We are dried up and with each passing day, it's getting costlier."

"Vijay, I know what you are trying to say, but try to understand – people know her after the magazine article. She won't be comfortable in a general ward. Even I have been receiving calls regarding her case," Dr Raza said.

"Why is that?" I asked.

"Because everyone knows that any publicity is good publicity..." He sighed.

He continued, "...And one more thing Vijay, shifting her to a general ward will not help you much, because the main cost of the treatment is the antibiotic, which will continue."

•

Dad came to see me at the hospital every alternate day. We used to sit in the cafeteria and discuss our problems. Money was a major issue now.

One evening, Dad came to the hospital. From a distance, it looked like he was dressed in a police uniform. But when he came closer, I realized it was slightly darker in colour, and its cap had two swords. He had a black coloured belt and an empty revolver case dangling down this waist. He had a badge which read 'SSL Security'. It was difficult to digest, but it was clear that he had joined a security company.

"How is my new uniform?" My father said, smiling in spite of all the pain.

"Dad, you are working as a security guard!"

"No, I am the head of security. You know, forty persons have to report to me. Never in my police career was I in charge of so many people. But look, here I am the boss. And..." He said with a proud face. "...And this dress looks cool on me. Don't you think I am looking a bit young?" He tried to lighten the environment.

My heart was filled with guilt. I could see how badly I had failed as a son.

"And Vijay, you know, I am paid more than an inspector."

"But Dad..." I tried to say something.

"I want to have a cup of tea with my son," he said ignoring my objection.

I went to the cafeteria and ordered two cups of tea. He said, "You know Vijay, yesterday something strange happened. Your mother apologized to me."

"Really! Mom said sorry to you?" I almost laughed as it was very rare for my mother to apologize to someone.

"At midnight, she woke me up and said she wanted to say something. She said she was sorry for all the fights she had with me, you and Astha."

I could see that he was a happy man in that moment.

"Throughout our life, we kept chasing useless things and stayed deprived of the joy of life," my father said.

"Dad, we will fight this problem together."

●

I explored every possible option to arrange the money in the next twenty-four hours. It was all in vain and at the end of the day, I had given up. I called each and every person I knew for help, but no one was ready or rich enough to help me. I made a few calls to financial lenders and banks, but everyone denied issuing a loan to an ad hoc assistant professor.

I decided to discuss the matter directly with the patient. I sat on the edge of her bed.

"Astha, I want to talk to you about something," I said.

"What? Tell me," she asked casually.

"I think this hospital isn't good enough to handle your treatment. Maybe I should consult someone at AIIMS. They have the top medical practitioners in the country. What do you say?" I said while hiding the actual reason from her.

She knew me too well to be fooled by that. "If you think that would be best for me, I am sure it would be. But Vijay, please don't hide anything from me. Is money the real issue?"

"Astha... No... It's not like that... It's..." I tried to make something up, but could not come up with anything.

"Vijay, tell me honestly," she asked firmly.

"Yes... You are right."

"Vijay, I know you love me beyond measure. You would do anything for me, but please accept the fact that even if everything goes well, there isn't much time left for me. So don't be too hard on yourself," she said and cupped my face in her palms. At times, it felt like I was the victim and she will be living the life after me.

"Don't say such stupid things. We will have a family, and we will live happily ever after."

"Okay, I will do whatever you say, but you have to promise me something," she said.

"What's that?"

"Whenever I die, I don't want you to cry in front of me. At the time of my departure, you should be standing with a smile. Even if it is a fake one."

I hugged her softly. We were silent; only our eyes were talking to each other.

My phone rang just then and I took the call.

"Hello sir," I answered instantly. It was the principal of the college.

"Hello Vijay, how are you and how is Astha doing?" he asked.

"Fine sir."

"Where are you? I want to meet you."

"Sir, I am in the hospital. I cannot come to the office. What's the matter?" I asked wondering why my principal wanted to meet me.

"Vijay, I am calling from the hospital reception."

"In the hospital? Please stay there. I'll be there in a minute," I said.

I disconnected the call, and asked Astha if she wanted to meet the principal. She didn't want to.

I nodded and left the room. My head was flooded with doubts.

Why has the principal come here? Has he come here to meet Astha? Was he planning to sack me? But for sacking me, he does not need to be here. My mind was abuzz with thoughts.

I found him sitting on a chair near the reception, waiting for me.

"Hello sir," I said.

"Hello Vijay. I am here to see Astha."

"She is not well, sir. Actually, after the magazine story, there has been a rush of visitors. The doctors have advised against it." I spoke up my mind without hesitation.

"No problem, I can understand," he said. "...Vijay, I didn't even wish her a happy birthday. I owe her a present, and I am here to give you the present."

"Gift? I don't understand," I said.

"Yes, a birthday gift," he said

This was the first time I had seen the human side of my principal that has always been hidden. It revealed that no one was completely bad.

"Here you go. A small gift from all of us." He handed me an envelope.

I opened it. It was a cheque of fifty lakhs issued in the name of Astha Sharma!

"Sir... This... I..." I spluttered. Was I dreaming?

"Vijay , your mother is a good friend of mine. I know your situation."

"Thanks sir, but this amount is huge for a principal."

"Yes, this amount is impossible for a principal alone, but very small for five thousand students. Very small against their love for their teacher."

"Thank you... Thank you very much, sir..." I realized that it wasn't a dream. My eyes were flooded with tears all of a sudden.

"I didn't do anything Vijay. The day you announced her birthday, I got pressure from other staff members to help you. Under their pressure and on your mother's request, I decided to publish her story. You know when Astha's story got published, every day, I found a group of students shouting in front of my office. They all had only one request. 'Please help Vijay sir'." He patted my back.

"It's really amazing." What else could I have said?

"That is why this amount is a gift of love."

"Thank you sir." I was tight-lipped because my eyes welled up. Only I could understand what that money meant to me. "Sir, I can't thank you enough for all the things you've done for me," I said, overwhelmed

He got up from his chair, about to leave. "I am sorry for the day I mistreated you. I had no idea about your problems," he said.

"Sir..." I tried to say something, but he had left. I kept on staring at his back until he was out of sight.

●

"Astha, the principal came to hand over your birthday gift. You know, this is a gift from my five thousand students."

She opened the envelope with a doubtful expression. "No, this is not possible." She could not believe it. "Fifty lakh rupees in my name."

"This is a real cheque. Now don't you dare say that you don't want charity."

"I know... I know. But believe it or not, that's what just happened."

I shrugged.

"And you know, I had a dream that one day, I'll own half a crore," she said with a smile. "How weird is that!"

I thought of her wishes and went outside and I texted my father:

Papa, my score is four out of seven.

34

After many sleepless nights and endless days, I took a night off. I was relaxed. Not that my problem was solved, but the positive response of people had given me some peace.

After going through hell, I found out that the world was a mixed bag of good and bad. I thanked life for giving me a chance. I was happy even in such a critical situation, and a peaceful smile sat on my face. When you have gone through the worst, small problems seem too small to upset you. But happiness and I were enemies. How could I be happy for long?

A team of doctors came for their routine check-up. Astha was not feeling well. She looked pale. Her breathing problem had worsened. Her labour pain was increasing exponentially, that too in an unusual way. Seeing the team of doctors, I stiffened as I didn't know what I'd be hearing.

They had a thick file of her reports and progress with them. The doctors were chatting and nodding, but they did not seem happy.

"How are you Astha?" asked one among the doctors.

"My legs, chest, and back hurt. I am feeling weak and drowsy," she said with much effort.

"It is because of the problems in breathing. You will need to use oxygen masks more often. It will lessen your strain around the chest. We are introducing some medicines that will make you sleep more for the time being."

She nodded in consent. She was content to spend the rest of her time sleeping while I was aware of the everlasting sleep that was just days away. I didn't know what to do or say.

The seriousness on Dr Raza's face was killing me. He called me inside the cabin after the examination. I guessed there was bad news, and the presence of all the five doctors just confirmed my assumption.

"What's wrong, doctor?" I was terrified.

"Vijay, please try to understand," Dr Raza said, "We took every possible care with the best facilities and doctors being provided to her."

He paused. I was sure it wasn't the first time he had such a situation in front of him, but his sorry face revealed his attachment to this case.

"Doctor, I am up for anything."

"Vijay, Astha has to go for a caesarean," said Dr Rachna.

"What are her chances of recovery after the operation?" I directly asked the question that mattered the most.

"Astha's condition is not good. Her resistance power is low, and her CD4 counts are decreasing day by day. We are pretty sure that her body does not have enough strength to heal after the operation. We will give her anesthesia to perform the operation, but we are not sure if she will regain consciousness."

"Suppose she wakes up after the operation?"

"Vijay, during the operation, she will lose a lot of blood. Her body will demand strength to heal and come back to consciousness. During or after the operation, she can slip into a coma, or even..." Dr Raza only managed to say that.

"Is there any chance?"

"I cannot make any promises."

I lost my reasons to fight. There were no tears in my eyes; I had been somewhat prepared for this. I looked through every eye present in the room, but none had any hope for me. The best I could find was sympathy, and I hated it.

"Thank you, doctor." Since I couldn't ask them to get lost, this was the best thing I could figure out to say to them and yet they found their meaning in it.

"Vijay," Dr Raza interrupted me.

I remained seated at my place and passed a look which said 'any-other-bad-news?"

"You did not ask anything about your baby."

Astha was the only thing that I cared for. I know it's hard to understand, but that's the truth.

Dr Raza brought me back to reality. His interruption made me realize that I had another bad news to listen to.

"Ohh, tell me in one go, doctor. Please." I was irritated.

"We are not even sure if Astha is going to deliver a healthy child. There's no way to find out if the child is HIV-infected or not. Sometimes HIV infection takes years to pass on to the child. So nothing could be said about the baby."

"When is the operation?"

"Her due date for delivery is after three days. But if she develops labour pain early, then we will have to operate immediately."

I wanted to get away from the room. I managed to say 'thanks' and they understood the rest.

●

I locked myself in the hospital washroom. I opened all the taps and cried on top of my voice. I felt like I had lost the battle. My eyes and nose were choked. I was boiling with anger and frustration. When the tears had dried, I decided to face my wife. The washroom mirror told me not to go with that face in front of her. My red eyes would reveal everything, and I didn't want her to know what I knew.

I came out from the washroom and waited for a few more minutes to calm my inner rage. I had a glass of water and moved to face my lovely wife. I opened the door to find her breathing with the help of an oxygen mask. As she saw me, she removed her oxygen mask and greeted me with a smile.

If Astha can smile after facing all this, how can you not? I reasoned with myself. I tried to smile fictitiously, but if you have a loving wife, it's difficult to hide anything, especially the pain.

"What happened, Vijay? Your eyes are going against your smile."

"I am fine; just something fell into my eyes," I said and pretended to clean them with a handkerchief. "Hey Astha, I think, we should name our baby."

"How about Aprajita?" she said instantly as if she had been waiting for this question.

"What does it mean?"

"Aprajita means a winner. The one who cannot be defeated." I smiled.

"What if we have a boy?"

"Am I dying soon?"

"What a stupid question is that?"

"If we have a baby boy, then I will decide his name after the delivery. But I am sure about Aprajita."

My mind said, *Aprajita means a winner. Astha will go down as a winner.* Something unusual struck me. I didn't know if it was a logical thing to do, but I decided to go with it. I excused myself and went to meet Dr Raza, for a last favour to fulfil her last wish.

"Dr Raza, I need a favour."

"Tell me what we can do for you," he said humbly. When a doctor cannot do anything good for you, they behave humble.

"Do you know acting?"

"I am a doctor."

35

She was going to die soon, and I had no idea how I would be able to manage everything. I was going through the toughest phase of my life and each passing day was tougher than the previous one. All the moments I spent with her were flashing in front of my eyes. Those beautiful memories of us being together.

I spent the night thinking. How could Astha always be cheerful and make the house a happy place to live? How she tried to cook something new every weekend. How she danced while cooking in the kitchen. How she had been shouting at her boss. How she forced me to eat eggs. Such a happy girl who brought life into the house.

I got up in the middle of the night and looked at her. She was sleeping with an oxygen mask on. Watching her sleep gave me a little peace. I took a sleeping pill, and slept like a corpse. The truth was, I never wanted to get up.

Next morning, when I got up, she was sleeping peacefully. I was thankful for the doctor's medicine. Only my parents and Sargam knew the truth. Dr Raza came in for a routine check-up with his team and Astha woke up. I wanted to know if Dr Raza had to say something. After a few minutes, Dr Raza looked at another doctor in the eyes and nodded.

"See doctor, there is a surprising improvement in her condition," Dr Raza said.

"It's excellent news," one doctor from his team replied.

"Yes, and there is an improvement in her haemoglobin and CD4 level too. CD4 count is more than 500 cells/mm^3," said Dr Rachna. I didn't belong to a medical background, so I was not able to understand the things they were saying. I was happy to see the love of my life smiling.

"It's a miracle. I am seeing this for the first time in my life," Dr Raza looked delighted.

"Is there any good news, doctor?" I was excited.

"Please wait a minute, Vijay," Dr Raza told his team. "Please proceed. I will be joining you later."

"There is hope. She's responding to our treatment well. The reports from the last night and today are incredible. These results are so good that I am hoping for a miracle."

"Really? Does that mean you can cure her?" I knew that it wasn't curable, but there was hope.

"I think she can deliver a healthy baby and recover after that. I don't know whether she can be completely cured or not."

"Will she have a c-section or a normal delivery?"

"She's too weak to have a healthy delivery. But looking at these results, I am sure there won't be any complications after the operation. Vijay, you have to get two donors of O+ blood group. We might need that at the time of surgery."

I looked at Astha. She had a smile on her face. I couldn't express how happy I was. I thanked the doctor. I was content. Dr Raza and Dr Rachna left the room. I came out to thank them.

"Vijay, people come to us with hope. Many times we fail to help the patients. Even a single failure hurts us. It's the first time in my life that I have felt so right after lying to someone." He took a deep breath and for the first time, I saw tears in Dr Raza's eyes.

●

I went outside for some fresh air. I had hardly walked a few steps when I was surprised to see a familiar handsome investment banker waiting. I have known this person and hated him from my heart because of many reasons. After all, I am a husband. I met him once, but I almost knew everything about him. I didn't know why he was there. His presence made me feel awkward. I went to him and said, "How come you are here, Mr Daniel?"

36

Daniel speaks

*B*efore this husband-wife duo stamp me a villain, allow me to introduce myself and narrate my version of the story.

I first met Astha in the fifth grade. She was very studious and a highly ambitious girl. She would always compete with me during the exams, but never succeeded. She always wished to be the topper of the class, but would end up coming second or third. I belong to a modern orthodox family. Modern to the outer world, and orthodox to the family. Sunday church visits are a ritual for my family. Come hell or high water, the visit would not be missed. Morning and evening prayers are an integral part of our routine. My mother was a homemaker. Marico India paid enough for us to be classified as a prosperous family with a decent standard of living.

A boy requires no reason to fall for a girl like her. She was a very demanding girlfriend. Astha's expensive shopping and dresses would irritate me because I had to pay for all of it. The only way to make her happy was buying her expensive gifts. Initially I considered it to be a price to be paid for having such a gorgeous girlfriend.

Astha's good look further decayed her senses. She aspired to be a model. According to me, it was foolish of her to even dream of being a model, given the kind of family she hailed from. This was my weird Astha.

Astha loved Salman Khan and had a wish to marry him, making me super jealous of him. I always wished he'd get married soon. In spite of all the hatred I had for Salman's script-less movies, I had no choice but to watch all of them, first day first show.

Astha had had a rough personal life. Owing to all her struggles, she had become a snob. The word 'apology' had no meaning for her. She had once demanded for pocket money from her stepmother and upon being refused, she had fought with her. That was the day I promised myself to fund her expenses. A poor guy like me who was trapped in her love during school days was definitely falling more in love with her each day.

I dreamt big for myself. I wished to pursue MBA from the USA. I broke the news of requiring huge amount in dollars to pursue MBA only to realize that my father had lost his job. Somehow I managed to fund myself while my dream girl landed a PO job at Axis Bank. Finally she had done something sensible by accepting this offer.

My real struggle commenced after a year in the USA when I learnt that my mother had had a minor heart attack, resulting in a bypass surgery which required a few lakh rupees. I requested Astha to issue a personal loan in my father's name. Being a PO at Axis Bank, this was a minuscule task for her. She gladly accepted my request and visited my place to get some papers signed by my father. I wish I hadn't asked her for this favour in the first place, because I was unaware of what my father would be saying to her.

"Daniel, your family is very orthodox. I think it is better to call off our relationship." She called me up and said this after she got home from my place. I tried to pacify her but couldn't spend long hours on phone owing to the costly ISD call rates. Out of the blue, her number was indefinitely switched off.

Astha's father had left for his heavenly abode. I concluded that she must be sad because of the unforeseen news. Little did I know that she was a psycho. When I got back to Delhi, I learnt that Astha had been married off to a rich professor. My girl, who had been mine for years, was now gone. I had no authority to address her as mine. I was fuming with anger. All I wanted was revenge. The thought of Astha sleeping in her husband's arms was intolerable to me. I vowed never to forgive her.

I still remember the day when I almost threw Vijay out of my house. I was jealous of him, and my jealousy turned into hatred after some time. I was living in an imaginary world, a world far away from reality. When I came to know that Vijay was nothing but an ordinary professor, I was amused. Seeing your enemy suffer is one of the most pleasant things. Thinking that Astha didn't have any luxuries helped to heal the wounds. I finally had my revenge. I always failed to understand that if Vijay was such a disaster, then why did she refuse to marry me? Was it because of my religion?

I tried to find out what exactly my father said to her when she visited my house. My father didn't reply, but I got my reply. My family pushed me to marry someone. I met a couple of girls. A successful banker, who looks good, was definitely a temptation for many useless girls. My family made me meet many girls who desperately wanted to have a lifetime guarantee like me. I don't know why, but I couldn't convince myself to marry any of them.

One Sunday I was sitting alone and thinking why I didn't want to marry any of them. My heart had the answer. I was still in love with Astha, or I wanted someone better than her. In reality, in an extreme corner of my heart, I wanted to show her that I deserve better than her, far better than her.

The reason for her decision to marry Vijay was not good enough for me to forgive her, but what I failed to understand was that when she decided not to marry me, she could have told me. We were together for more than ten years. That was the internal struggle that I had. In a war between the heart and the mind, my mind won. After all, I am an investment banker. She didn't deserve my forgiveness; if she was really apologetic, she should have called me at least once. Not send her loser husband. The more stupid one was her husband; how could he come to meet her wife's ex-boyfriend. A normal human won't do it. Either he was way too dumb or Astha was too dominating.

One day I went to a bookstore and picked up a magazine I wanted and suddenly noticed the cover of another magazine. I saw a familiar face on the cover. The same face that had made me lose my sleep. A smile to die for. The cover read:

A truly inspiring and eye-opening story of a pregnant HIV positive woman – Page-16

I started to read the story. It was about the woman I hated more than anything. But after reading all that, I had tears in my eyes. I could not sleep that night. I realized that Vijay was right; she wasn't well. That moment I realized what a loving husband that guy was. The next day was a Sunday. I decided to attend the church and make a confession.

"Father I took my revenge from somebody I hated a lot. Did I do the right thing?" This was my question from the confession box.

"What do you think? Are you happy?"

"Yes, father. I am happy," I answered.

"If you are happy, then why are you here?"

I realized I had limited time to correct myself. I had to right my wrong. I was a loser because I was the one who had retaliated, and only a loser retaliates.

37

Daniel Speaks II

I now knew everything about Astha and I felt truly sorry for her. Somewhere, deep down, an ache in my heart rose up sharply. I reached the hospital the next day but couldn't man up to see her. I could feel tides of the love racing through my heart again. It was impossible for me to go into her room. I saw Vijay coming out. He recognized me and started walking towards me.

"What brings you here, Mr Daniel?" he asked me politely.

"Hi, Vijay. How is Astha?"

"She is fine." The misery in his eyes said otherwise.

"Sorry, Vijay. I am very sorry for my behaviour. I was angry and didn't know. But..." It was hard to complete that sentence, but that man had been on a rollercoaster ride in the ocean of sorrow and hope.

"It's okay Daniel, I understand."

"Vijay, can I see her?"

"Astha doesn't want to see anyone."

"Vijay, I have known her for more than ten years. It's important for me to meet her. It's something personal; it isn't about sympathy."

Vijay didn't speak for a few minutes. On a different note, it was very awkward that I was seeking someone's permission to meet Astha. I still remember how I never asked to visit her home. I was never welcomed at her place, but I never cared.

"*Come with me.*"

It was weird that I was going to meet my ex-girlfriend with her husband. The situation couldn't have been weirder. There was a flower shop outside the hospital. Vijay purchased a small bouquet of seven flowers with a few lilies and sunflowers.

"Daniel, take these. Congratulate her on becoming a mother. Don't tell her anything about our meeting and don't mention anything related to her disease," he briefed me. I nodded.

"What about you?"

"I have a few things to sort out. I will be back in an hour."

I moved forward to see Vijay's Astha. Every step towards her swayed a new set of emotions inside. I halted for a minute at her door. I was going to see the girl I loved and hated the most at the same time. There was a strange enthusiasm to meet her; inspite of hating her from every corner of my heart, I was still desperate to see her. We human beings are hypocrites. Even I can understand those feelings, but I don't want to mention them here. After all, its Vijay's book.

Utterly confused, I decided to enter her room and talk to her. I saw her sleeping with an oxygen mask on. I was taken aback. A tear rolled down my cheeks. It was hard to believe that she was the same girl who had been so beautiful. It was the same girl for whom I have had fallen a million times. I desperately wanted to hug her, but how could I.

"Hi, Astha." My voice woke her up. I looked at her beautiful face

"Daniel? Am I dreaming?" She removed the oxygen mask.

"It's so weird to see you like this," I realized that I could not afford to sympathize. "Congratulations Astha. You are going to be an excellent mother. I brought these flowers for you," I said as cheerfully as I could.

"Did Sargam tell you that I am hospitalized or anyone else?" She guessed herself. It pleased me that the girl I had loved had not changed a bit. She told me to adjust her bed. She wanted to talk to me properly.

"You have not changed at all. You still ask questions and then answer them on your own. Are you happy with your marriage?" I asked teasingly.

"Yes, I am very happy. You know, I am married to a great guy. My husband is a wealthy man. He is the HOD at Sriram College. He earns a lot. I am thinking of quitting my job to concentrate on the kid."

"Aha! He's the HOD there?"

"Yes," she didn't say anything for some time. "So, you are a rich man now, Daniel."

"No, I am the same loser," I replied.

"You were never a loser, Daniel. Your dad talked me into not marrying you. He had his reasons. When I had been to your place, your father literary pleaded to me. I was struggling then, I didn't want more struggles in my life. This was the reason I decided to marry Vijay so quickly. I wanted to get over with my stupid life struggles. You are not a loser, Daniel. You are an amazing human being. I know you will find someone a lot better than me."

"Of course, Astha. I deserve a better girl than you and I shall find her."

"I am so sorry Daniel. It was the toughest call that I ever made in my life," she said.

"Don't be sorry. I know it was hard for you."

"Enough with the past. Tell me about your new life. Does your bank pay well? I know it must be a few lakhs every month."

"Look at you! Still asking the questions and answering them on your own. I am not answering that. What about your husband? Where is he?"

"He has a very important meeting to attend at his college. The hectic admission season is on. The college offers a five lakh commission for every admission in management quota and my husband brings in one entry every year."

"What if he got caught one day?"

"Nothing. Many colleges want to hire him. He's a wanted man. He will join anyone of them." Yes, she hadn't changed a bit. She was the same girl that I loved madly.

"Well, I know that. Your husband is indeed an amazing man. I don't doubt that."

"How do you know him?"

"Vijay came to my house once."

"Why did he go to your house?"

"Vijay had come to apologize on your behalf. He said Astha was apologetic about her decision to marry him."

She was in a state of shock and her jaw fell.

"You know Astha, since the day I knew you were married to Vijay, I hated you with everything I've got. Maybe, I would have killed you for betraying me if I happened to see you. From that day onwards, I only wanted to see you in pain. When I met your professor husband, I felt happy that he was your husband. I considered him a total disaster."

"Don't you dare speak about him that way," she said in an intense tone.

"Astha, when I came to know about your condition, my heart was filled with respect for the husband who had walked up to me to apologize on behalf of his wife." I found my throat chocked. I took a glass of water.

"And today, when I know that it was just his decision to apologize, I pity myself." I sighed. "Astha, you don't need to apologize for anything. You have married a person like him; it hardly matters if he is a professor or an HOD. He may *not be earning as much as me, but as a human being, he is a gem of a person."*

"Oh, Daniel."

"Astha, during our school days, you always wanted to be on top. But I defeated you in every exam. If life is an exam, then this time you have defeated me. You are the winner Astha and will always be one. I have money, a job, a car, a flat and everything, but I am still a loser, because I don't have the best person with me."

Astha was silent. It was difficult to see a beautiful pregnant mother in tears. I decided to end this conversation.

I was about to move out, but suddenly I realized that this would be the last time I'd be seeing her. It was hard to accept for me, but an awkward eagerness held me back. I didn't know whether it was permissible to do that, but I did. In a blink, I got close to her and hugged her. We were both in tears, and I kept saying, "Please forgive me, please forgive me, Astha, please forgive me."

38

I can sense that he still loved Astha. I hesitated to his request to meet Astha. But I wanted this meeting to happen. One, he was the first love of her life and second, Daniel's name was mentioned in her wish list. I would do anything to fulfil Astha's wishes, even if it meant for her to meet her ex-boyfriend.

After dropping him with her, I left the room, but could not go away. I occupied the seat closest to the door and tried to overhear the conversation. I had heard a little conversation, which an inferior husband in love can understand. I know I am a selfish man, but there is nothing wrong in being a selfish person. And this could be a chance to know something more about Astha.

Daniel came out of the room after some time; he wasn't looking the same. I waited for some time before I went inside to see Astha. I didn't want to see tears in her eyes. Astha was almost asleep. I did not disturb her. I took a seat and just kept looking at her. It was satisfying to see her sleep peacefully. I was thinking, she will yell at me once she wakes up and will demand an answer as to why I went to meet Daniel. All kind of thoughts had started to come to my mind when she opened her eyes.

"Why are you staring at me like that"? Astha asked.

"You were sleeping, I thought."

"No, I was awake. You were staring at me and thinking about something. What was that?"

"Thinking about our baby and the lovely future with you by my side."

She smiled and extended her arms to hug me. I hugged her. In a few moments, I found myself kissing her until I felt some warm droplets on my hand. Her eyes were all moist.

Before I could start to console her she, demanded, "I want to meet Sargam." She did not mention Daniel or his visit, despite knowing the fact that I was aware about their meeting at the hospital. It was a strange call, but I didn't want to argue with her. It was a surprise that she wanted to meet Sargam at this time, but I didn't say anything and called her. I felt good to have someone else around her. Sargam was there in an hour. I updated her on the situation. She could be called for the operation anytime now. Sargam nodded. I went outside for some fresh air. Select Citywalk mall was nearby, and I decided to get lost somewhere in the crowd. There was a big chaos outside a shop, and I was amazed by the power of the drink. It was a common site outside a government liquor shop. Many daily worshippers of the great nectar were standing outside. I failed to understand why there was such a huge rush. My close observation answered me, half of them were drinking also. The government made rules, but failed to control the consumption of liquor at public places. On the contrary, the government is involved by taking the charge of the distribution. A police staff was there. His presence was futile; he himself soaked under the nectar.

"One bottle of Signature," I asked.

"Khambha?" asked the seller.

"No… half," I said.

I paid three hundred rupees and headed home to Malviya Nagar. I had tried liquor only once before and hadn't liked the taste. But today, I needed something to lighten me up, because this pain in my head… in my heart… my life… it was getting unbearable.

I reached home and crumbled on the sofa. I poured myself an extra-large drink out of the half and mixed it with the semi-frozen Coke from the refrigerator. I was a novice at making a drink. I pushed down half of it in one go. It tasted horrible. I emptied another glass after a few minutes. My mind started receiving the little swing for which I had invested three hundred bucks.

I felt better with the booze inside me. I was amazed at how drinking can give strength to face people. Why Astha had always craved for this. Why my mother protested when she found Astha drinking at home. Meanwhile I had finished one more peg. I started to feel like I was in a garden. I closed my eyes and allowed my head to follow the train of thoughts.

What next? What next after Astha? What if the baby is also diagnosed positive with the disease? How this room was lively with her smile. I thought about her crazy wishes. Why did Astha want to marry a hero? I looked at the mirror. Do I look like a hero? No, this face belong to a zero. Yes, I know this zero.

I think alcohol had started fulfiling its duty.

I looked at my reflection in the mirror and saw a person who had lost a battle.

After some time, I passed out on the sofa. The metallic ringtone of my cell welcomed a new day of struggle. It was Sargam.

"Hello, Sargam. What happened?"

"Vijay, I need to leave, something important has come up. How much time will you need to get here?"

"You can leave, Sargam. I'll be there in ten minutes."

I disconnected the call and dressed in a hurry, and popped in a mouth-freshener and soaked myself with a deodorant.

I was about to move to the hospital when I looked at the bottle. It was like the bottle was telling me not to leave it behind. It was her favourite, after all. I packed that half-filled bottle and thanked my mind. It was still working perfectly. I started my car and headed towards the hospital.

By the time I reached there, Sargam had already left.

When I reached her room, I found Astha in pain.

"Astha! What happened? Are you alright?"

"I think the time has come."

I nodded. I was blank. I didn't know how to react to her answer, but she asked another question.

"Are you drunk?"

"Yes, I tried a few sips; it tasted horrible. How do you like—"

I was cut short by a sudden surge of pain. *"Call the doctor now, Vijay!"*

I rushed to call the doctor. A junior doctor was on shift and examined Astha. He told us that she would need to be operated upon within an hour. He left the room after performing some medical procedures. A nurse came with a green apron dress and said, "She has to wear this."

"Okay." I nodded.

After ten minutes, the nurse came out and told me that Astha was not allowed to eat anything. She asked important questions from the operation checklist like the blood arrangement, etc.

Before leaving, the nurse said, "You have half an hour."

I could not feel anything when the nurse said that. She meant after half an hour, I would lose my love...my life. I started shivering at the thought. I went outside and stood there for quite some time. I felt that I could not see anything because my eyes were swollen up with tears. I tried to calm down and splashed some chilled water from the water cooler over my face. I couldn't waste the next half an hour crying – the most precious thirty minutes of my life. I looked into the mirror and forced a smile.

Astha was dressed in green and her hair was clipped. I closed the door from inside.

"Hey, can you feel the baby?" I asked holding her hand.

"Yes." She was gasping in pain.

"You know, we will have the best news of our life in just a couple of hours."

She didn't say a word and just smiled. I lifted her bed with the help of the automatic pullers. She was now sitting at an angle.

"Let's have a party." I placed the hospital glass on the table and took out a liquor bottle from my bag. I served a large peg for myself and half a glass of water for her.

"You can have whiskey. I'll just stick to water. Remember everything has changed."

"But you won't act like Vijay," I said.

I added five drops of whiskey to her glass. I was ready for the last party of my life.

"Why so little whiskey in my glass? You have just added five drops," she asked softly. I had added just five drops because my score was five and it was the only reason to celebrate.

"You are not allowed to drink. Five drops to give colour to your peg. No more discussion. Cheers."

"No, please add two more drops," she said in pain. I didn't want to argue with her and added two drops without much fuss.

I made her the last peg and said, "You are the winner, Astha."

"No, *we* are the winners. Cheers to the winners."

"Cheers." I emptied the glass of whiskey. She only tasted the last peg of the colored liquid.

I came close to her and softly placed a gentle kiss on her cheeks and then someone knocked at the door.

"Two minutes," I screamed.

"Okay sir." I heard a nurse reply.

I looked deep into her eyes. Her face had a smile of a winner and on the contrary, I had tears in my eyes.

"How are you feeling?"

"Finally, I have found my inner peace. I am happy, but I want a promise Vijay." Her tears told me she was lying.

"Yeah, tell me?"

"This is the last time we drink. We won't drink after this day; it's not good for anything."

"It's a promise." I considered asking why, but I didn't.

I could sense her urge to live more. She wanted to enjoy life, but we were helpless. The worst thing that can happen to anyone is knowing that your loved one is dying with each passing second and you can do nothing about it. You cannot change their destiny. You cannot change the truth. Her labour pain grew to an unbearable level. I managed to hide the liquor bottle quickly before opening the door. I went near her, kissed her forehead, and cried silently. I was flooded with emotions and wanted to say a million things, but said, "Love you, and you are the best wife."

She summoned her courage and said, "Love you too, and you are the best husband."

39

Astha had been moved to the operation theater. I came back and bolted the door of her room from the inside. My mind stopped working and I felt like I had lost everything that was mine in this world. I realized that the signature bottle still had some left. But I refused to push it down my throat. I summoned my courage and dialled Papa.

"Hello, Papa."

"Hi, Vijay." I was about to speak but found it difficult to utter a word. "What happened beta? Has Astha gone for the operation?"

"Papa, I am missing you." Was the only audible thing that came out of my mouth before I disconnected the call and my body started shivering. I opened the door and collapsed on the bed where Astha had been lying. Rapid tears drained my cheeks. With every passing second, the alcohol in me was winning over. Half a bottle was not enough, but for a person like me who never drinks, it's more than enough.

Constantly shivering, I repeatedly kept saying: "Love you, Astha. I love you." I don't know when I sunk into an unconscious state.

•

I woke up to find three people standing in the room.

"Papa, what happened? Is Astha okay?" Despite knowing the answer, I asked almost foolishly.

"You are blessed with a baby girl." My father said without an emotion crossing his face. Even then, only Astha was on my mind.

"Papa…"

"Vijay, Astha will always be alive in our hearts."

Suddenly, the truth lay naked in front of me. For the last six months, I had been running past the truth and finally the bitter truth of my life was right there, staring me in the face. I was prepared for this. My father kept talking, but I was as far from his words as his face from emotions. My complete life was flashing in front of me, going through in frames. I was not crying. I was so shocked that I didn't know what that state was. A state in which your senses fail you and it's hard to react to even a grave danger. My father looked towards Sargam.

"Vijay, this is Astha's last letter for you."

I knew Astha could not write a letter; it was written by Sargam. Now I understood why Sargam was suddenly summoned at that hour.

Hi Vijay,

I wanted to say millions of things to you. But you know, it was not possible to speak because I did not wish to depart in tears. What I am going to write here, I mean from the bottom of my heart. A dying person never tells a lie.

These doctors never talked about anything in front of me and suddenly one day they behaved like they had seen the biggest breakthrough. I could sense their acting. But you were not aware that one day Dr Raza had come and informed me that I am going to deliver a female child. A doctor only does that if the pregnancy is at risk. This is how I realized that my life was coming to an end. I have always known the truth. The day you first used a condom, I had a suspicion that something was not quite right. On my last day at office, the guard told me you were there at the office. Your frequent visit to your father's place added fuel to the fire. One day I asked your father and he couldn't lie; he told me about the disease. Throughout the night I was thinking how a pregnant HIV patient would act. I couldn't help thinking how I could have been infected! The only cause I can think of is blood transfusion a couple of years back when I had been hospitalised for a severe allergy. And I was surprised that you never tried to find out! I can go peacefully, knowing how much you love me and trust me.

Vijay, throughout my life, I had lived in revenge and anger. Love and forgiveness were unfamiliar to me. I had a terrible family. Both, my pretentious stepmother and a cowardly father, never loved me much, so I ended up loving myself.

Whenever someone shared their mother's words and love, it hurt. I sat aside and cried whenever anyone mentioned their happy family. I didn't have any shoulder to lean on, so I spent many nights alone in tears. Although it may have placed me in a vulnerable state, crying with someone had always been healing. Finally, I found support in Daniel.

Daniel had a special place in my life. Though my need for a family was never fulfiled. I have always thought highly of myself, so I decided that one day I would become the best mom. Was that a choice made in anger and revenge? I don't know.

I always craved for a mother. Now I have one. I have everything. I have forgiven my mother, because she forced me to marry you. Yes, I am forgiving her.

Vijay, when I came to know that I am an HIV patient, I could not believe it and wondered how it was possible? What was the source of infection which is still not known to me?

I was amazed to know you never asked the reason.

You are a crazy husband who decided to fulfil my weird wishes that I had written when I was down with five pegs of vodka. Vijay, I lived for twenty-eight years on this earth. But what I enjoyed in my last seven months was amazing. The best portion of life is the small nameless moments you spend smiling with someone who matters the most to you. It was a rare feeling for me the way you cared for me and loved me. I had always thought I did wrong with Daniel. But he ended up forgiving me. My every dream and desire has been fulfiled. I will not be here tomorrow, but I am not carrying any grudges, or complaints, or even regrets.

I have lived a life of a winner. And I wanted to see my husband as a winner too.

Vijay, may be you are average in looks. You speak rarely. But you have proved that any good looking person may not be as beautiful, but a person with a golden heart is always beautiful. Vijay, you have to marry again and live like a winner. You have to marry not only for me, but also for our baby. I don't want my baby to struggle for a mother like her mother did. If my baby is diagnosed positive with HIV, then also you have to fight and wait till scientists find a cure to defeat this virus. I am sure one day humanity and love will win.

Vijay, it is a really great relief to see a confident person in you. But please don't break down after me. Our baby will keep on reminding you about this.

When I was in school, I had a crush on Salman. In class tenth, I had written a letter to him and Salman had posted me a photo with a message:

'To Astha, with love, Salman Khan.'

As time passed, my obsession with proving myself as one of the most beautiful looking people in the world heightened. I started believing that one day, I would marry a hero.

Then I married to a common man like you. I was not aware that you were a crazy man, who'd go to any extent just to keep me happy. That was the same thing a hero does in movies. He defeats the villain and gets his love. Today I have no one to defeat and I have many people to love. Vijay, you are not a common man. You are the superhero of my life.

Keep on fighting, my loving hero. Always try to represent yourself as happy, because initially it becomes your look, gradually it becomes your habit, and one day it becomes your personality.

Love,
Astha

40

I shifted back to Noida with my parents after a few days. Life was not the same. Everything had changed. Only one person made us alive – Aprajita. My mother was taking care of her. We often had lunch together. Astha had left, but had united my family. Now Astha had done her part, next was Aprajita. My father resigned from the temporary security job. He got his retirement back, but the inner peace was missing.

One evening, I was sitting on the sofa.

"Vijay," he said touching my shoulder. "Why don't you write a book?"

"What shall I write about?"

"Write about your Astha."

"I have never even written a poem, how can I write a book? And who will read the story of a loser?"

"You are not a loser, Vijay. What happened to those wishes which you were trying to accomplish?"

"Nothing much. I am happy that I tried." I heaved a sigh of relief, pulled the paper, and read:

Seven impossible wishes before I die:

1. Become a good mother
2. Sorry to Daniel
3. Marry a hero or celebrity.
4. A very grand birthday.
5. Having one or half-a-crore in my account.
6. Photo on front page of a gossip magazine
7. BB on me.

"Congratulations Papa! Your son's score is five out of seven."

"You score is six, not five."

I frowned. He brought Astha's last letter. He encircled a line and gave back to me.

"I have read this many times."

"Just read this line."

The encircled line: *'You are the hero of my life'*.

That was really weird. I held the paper and my mind guessed the situation in which she might have written that letter. I started assuming the conversation between Astha and Sargam. Why had Astha specifically mentioned this line. My father prodded.

"Vijay, what are you thinking?"

"Papa, Astha was aware that I was trying to fulfil her wishes. Astha has written this letter in order to give me an extra score."

"How can you say that?"

"Read this line: *'A dying person never tells a lie.'*"

"What is so special in it?"

"Papa, Astha need not explain that she is not lying to me. It means she had deliberately written this. She was lying."

My father was dumbstruck at my guess because I was right. A right guess always makes the wrong stupefied.

"Even if she had written it deliberately, you should understand her love for you."

If it was right, it was hard to believe. She was indeed a rare personality.

"Vijay, she wanted you to be a winner. She wanted you to accomplish her wishes. Anyway, you were chasing those wishes for your own self."

"But what about her last wish *'BB'*. I am sure she knew about her last wish too." I stood up to go and make a call to Sargam. My father held my hand.

"Vijay, I know what her last wish was."

I suddenly understood everything; how Astha had known about everything and who had plotted behind my back. I felt cheated but he was a father, a loving one at that.

"Papa, so you are the one who leaked things to her."

"Her last wish is," he ignored my question and said, "a Bestseller Book."

I thought for a few seconds and talked internally to my Astha. *You are really a weird wife.*

"What happened Vijay? Why are you so silent?"

"Papa, I have never written anything before."

"We will support you. Whoever loves Astha will give their version of the story, Vijay. You try, it hardly matters whether it will be a bestseller or not. Just go ahead, my son, and achieve seven out of seven."

I smiled at my father's efforts. Meanwhile, my mother handed the most beautiful gift to me.

I was holding a three-day-old baby. I was not in a position to guess whether she resembled me or Astha. The baby was looking like a cute gift from Astha. She was sleeping peacefully, giving me the same peace that was given by her mother. I wanted to see her with her eyes open. I stroked her face with my finger. It was really an awesome feeling to hold your own baby. That reminded me of something. I passed a weird smile.

"Why are you smiling like that?" my father prodded.

"I am trying to learn how to be 'happy'."

My father looked surprised. It was out of context. He must have been hoping to hear something about her last wish. With a weird smile I said, "Don't worry Papa. I will write a book. I will fulfil her last wish..."

41

Vijay's Father speaks
Acknowledgements

*D*ear reader,

I might be a rare father who is writing all this. Did you like the book? It has been written by my son. He thought he was a loser in life, but his wife changed him. Now your love for Vijay will help him to be a winner in real life too. Initially Vijay was struggling to write this, but later I realized publishing a book was another herculean task.

Anyway, since you have read the book, it means it has been published. I can't request you to buy this book to help my son. Plus, don't buy this book only to help my son. Buy it to read a story of love.

I am sure it will be a bestseller. I hope you got my message. I am a father, and am desperately waiting to see my son score a seven out of seven. Fulfiling her last wish is up to you.

Aprajita has been tested negative for HIV and we continue to struggle with our lives to make each other happy. You might be thinking about me. I am a happy father. A happy retired father... And you know what the best part of retirement is? To have a grandchild.